MW00776002

Over the River & Through the Woods

Clifford D. Simak

Over the River & Through the Woods

Clifford D. Simak

with an introduction by Poul Anderson

Tachyon Publications
Dark Regions Press

San Francisco, California

OVER THE RIVER AND THROUGH THE WOODS: THE BEST SHORT FICTION OF CLIFFORD D. SIMAK

Cover illustration by Michael Dashow

A Tachyon Publication
1459 18th Street #139
San Francisco, CA 94107

Published in conjunction with Dark Regions Press
P.O. Box 6301
Concord, CA 94524

Edited by Jacob Weisman

ISBN: 0-9648320-2-X

Printed in the United States of America

Permissions

Table of Contents

Introduction by Poul Anderson

Forgetfulness is a mark of these times. Deluged and obsessed with new input of every kind, although originality seems to get scarcer and scarcer, people let the work of the past drop from their minds. Soon it disappears from their bookstores, libraries, theaters, concert halls, and screens. Soon after that, younger people come along who have never heard of it. Oh, yes, there are enduring exceptions. You can still find Tolstoy, watch Shakespeare, or hear Beethoven. But—to name three writers well-known half a century ago—where now are Stephen Vincent Benét, James Branch Cabell, and Lord Dunsany? On my bookshelves, maybe on yours, but on how many more?

They did wonderful fantasy, among other things. The same water of Lethe laps through science fiction. Already such splendid makers of it as Alfred Bester, Henry Kuttner, Fritz Leiber, Catherine L. Moore, Clifford D. Simak, Cordwainer Smith, and Theodore Sturgeon are slipping into obscurity. Only trade paperbacks of some few of their books linger in print. It is mass market editions that attract new customers. What a pity that the next generation is missing out on the experiences that mine enjoyed. What a loss of example and inspiration to the creative talents of today.

I hope this isn't too dour an opening for a few remarks about Clifford Simak. That would be altogether inappropriate. The spirit in his stories is humane, tolerant, generally cheerful and optimistic. Mainly I want to explain why the revival of these stories you will find here is praiseworthy. May we see much more, along with the work of other giants. And let this happen not as solemn scholarship, but for fun. Let the new generation share the old pleasures. They remain as fresh as this morning's sunrise.

Also, to speak of the past is fitting in connection with Simak. His roots went deep. From them he drew the vividness and vitality of even his widest-ranging tales.

For instance, take his most famous book, *City*. Appearing in magazines over a period of years, when gathered together these narratives proved to be an epic spanning centuries and universes, the triumphs and tensions and tragedies and ultimate transcendence in humankind's many-branching destiny. Yet it is, throughout, a quiet epic, whether a scene be laid on the huge planet Jupiter or beside an anthill on Earth. Most of the action centers on a single old house, the Webster family who live there, the intelligent dogs who succeed them, and Jenkins, the robot who attends them all.

Nobody but Clifford Donald Simak could have written *City*. Born in Wisconsin in 1904, he became a journalist in Minneapolis, Minnesota, rising from reporter to a leading position on the editorial staff. A devoted husband and father as well, he couldn't have had a lot of spare time for writing science fiction. I have heard that he did it by sheer discipline. Each day at home he would go into his study, close the door, and devote at least one full hour to his latest story. Perhaps not a single word would come forth, but he spent that hour trying.

He was, in fact, a thorough professional. I remember well some advice he gave me early in my career. I was having a manuscript rejected everywhere because it was too long for its plot. "The way to shorten a story," he told me, "is to write the last part of it." This was said in pure helpfulness. He was never condescending or arrogant. Rather, he treated everyone, down to the lowliest neophyte writer or fan, as his equal, his neighbor. He listened more than he talked. To all of us he was just plain Cliff.

Not that he lacked salt. Once a colleague passed through Minneapolis. Cliff, Gordon Dickson, and I gave him lunch at a downtown restaurant. He was a jovial sort and the occasion went pleasantly. He was, though, an ardent socialist, who at one point made a claim about the impossibility of learning the truth from the kept American press. Cliff replied in his gentle fashion that he had been a newsman his whole working life, and had never seen a story censored or killed merely because somebody wouldn't like it. He paused, then added that he'd have to take that back. A while ago he'd been sent down to Kensington to do a piece on the runestone found there, allegedly left by medieval Norse explorers. He arrived with an open mind, carried out his research, and concluded it was a fake. "No," said his editor, "we can't print that in Minnesota!"

I will always regret not having seen more of Cliff than I did. He wasn't much for beer parties, conventions, or other such activities; he lived in a suburb, I in the city, and presently I moved to the West Coast. Afterward we exchanged a few letters and met in person now and then, cordially but briefly. Among my fondest memories is that of the last time. I was back in Minneapolis on business. Gordon Dickson and I took Cliff to dinner, and ended in my room talking with him for several hours. It was very good talk. He was at once down-to-earth and as civilized a person as I have ever known.

By then he was retired and widowed, but dauntlessly writing fiction full-time, and grand books those are. Ill health eventually put a stop to that. I don't believe anybody heard any complaint from him. He died in his sleep in 1988.

When he dealt with his Midwestern land and people, he was one of the finest regional writers the United States has had. He knew them, he *was* them, and he gave them to us in his own homely words, which he nevertheless made into poetry. A random example from *City*: "Dusk was falling, the dusk of early spring, a dusk that smelled of early pussy willows." You'll see many a comparable passage in the selections here. They don't usually lend themselves so readily to quotation. The Midwestern language is easygoing, understated, taking its time to make its point. But in Cliff Simak's hands, that point will reach to your heart.

By no means did he confine himself to his native soil. The yarns he spun can stretch to the ends of space-time and beyond. They can encompass other planets, cold light-years, non-human beings, high-tech machines, strange civilizations to come. More often than not, however, their protagonists bear the same basic, unpretentious strength and decency as himself and the folk from which he sprang. I don't think this is a failure of imagination; rather, it is profound insight. These values may be unfashionable nowadays, but they are not extinct and they will return, because they are the values by which we survive.

Please don't suppose from this that Cliff ever got preachy, florid, or otherwise dismal. He had a healthy streak of irreverence and a great sense of humor. Above all, he was a crackling hell of a storyteller. A glance over the contents of the present volume will show his variety.

"A Death in the House" expresses the ideal of kindliness, but unsentimentally and in the eerie context of a meeting with a creature totally alien.

"The Big Front Yard" again brings the cosmos home to our everyday world, a favorite motif of the author's, in a lighter vein. The pomposity and officiousness of certain people, governmental and local, come in for some wicked satire.

"Goodnight Mr. James" is a horror story, with the worst horror lying in the casual cruelty of a society not terribly unlike ours.

"Dusty Zebra" is hilarious.

"Neighbor" is Americana worthy of Mark Twain or John Steinbeck, though placed in Simak country.

"Over the River and Through the Woods" is low-key heartbreak.

"Construction Shack" is straight interplanetary science fiction—no, not quite. It will neatly lead you up the garden path and leave you there with a surprised grin on your face.

"The Grotto of the Dancing Deer" takes us back to present-day Europe and a prehistoric habitation. Cliff didn't really need cosmic settings to evoke the immensity of time. He could do it with as simple a prop as a bone flute.

These stories are a well-chosen sample. Plenty more Simak awaits rediscovery, both novels and shorter pieces. I hope this book will be not just a memorial but a beginning.

A Death In The House

Old Mose Abrams was out hunting cows when he found the alien. He didn't know it was an alien, but it was alive and it was in a lot of trouble and Old Mose, despite everything the neighbors said about him, was not the kind of man who could bear to leave a sick thing out there in the woods.

It was a horrid-looking thing, green and shiny, with some purple spots on it, and it was repulsive even twenty feet away. And it stank.

It had crawled, or tried to crawl, into a clump of hazel brush, but hadn't made it. The head part was in the brush and the rest lay out there naked in the open. Every now and then the parts that seemed to be arms and hands clawed feebly at the ground, trying to force itself deeper in the brush, but it was too weak; it never moved an inch.

It was groaning, too, but not too loud—just the kind of keening sound a lonesome wind might make around a wide, deep eave. But there was more in it than just the sound of winter wind; there was a frightened, desperate note that made the hair stand up on Old Mose's nape.

Old Mose stood there for quite a spell, making up his mind what he ought to do about it, and a while longer after that working up his courage, although most folks offhand would have said that he had plenty. But this was the sort of situation that took more than just ordinary screwed-up courage. It took a lot of foolhardiness.

But this was a wild, hurt thing and he couldn't leave it there, so he walked up to it and knelt down, and it was pretty hard to look at, though there was a sort of fascination in its repulsiveness that was hard to figure out—as if it were so horrible that it dragged one to it. And it stank in a way that no one had ever smelled before.

Mose, however, was not finicky. In the neighborhood, he was not well known for fastidity. Ever since his wife had died almost ten years before, he had lived alone on his untidy farm and the housekeeping that he did was the scandal of all the neighbor women. Once a year, if he got around to it, he sort of shoveled out the house, but the rest of the year he just let things accumulate.

So he wasn't as upset as some might have been with the way the creature smelled. But the sight of it upset him, and it took him quite a while before he could bring himself to touch it, and when he finally did, he was considerably surprised. He had been prepared for it to be either cold or slimy, or maybe even both. But it was neither. It was warm and hard and it had a clean feel to it, and he was reminded of the way a green corn stalk would feel.

He slid his hand beneath the hurt thing and pulled it gently from the clump of hazel brush and turned it over so he could see its face. It hadn't any face. It had an enlargement at the top of it, like a flower on top of a stalk, although its body wasn't any stalk, and there was a fringe around this enlargement that wiggled like a can of worms, and it was then that Mose almost turned around and ran.

But he stuck it out.

He squatted there, staring at the no-face with the fringe of worms, and he got cold all over and his stomach doubled up on him and he was stiff with fright—and the fright got worse when it seemed to him that the keening of the thing was coming from the worms.

Mose was a stubborn man. One had to be stubborn to run a runty farm like this. Stubborn and insensitive in a lot of ways. But not insensitive, of course, to a thing in pain.

Finally he was able to pick it up and hold it in his arms and there was nothing to it, for it didn't weigh much. Less than a half-grown shoat, he figured.

He went up the woods path with it, heading back for home, and it seemed to him the smell of it was less. He was hardly scared at all and he was warm again and not cold all over.

For the thing was quieter now and keening just a little. And although he could not be sure of it, there were times when it seemed as if the thing were snuggling up to him, the way a scared and hungry baby will snuggle to any grown person that comes and picks it up.

Old Mose reached the buildings and he stood out in the yard a minute, wondering whether he should take it to the barn or house. The barn, of course, was the natural place for it, for it wasn't human—it wasn't even as close to human as a dog or cat or sick lamb would be.

He didn't hesitate too long, however. He took it into the house and laid it on what he called a bed, next to the kitchen stove. He got it straightened out all neat and orderly and pulled a dirty blanket over it, and then went to the stove and stirred up the fire until there was some flame.

Then he pulled up a chair beside the bed and had a good, hard, wondering look at this thing he had brought home. It had quieted down a lot and seemed more comfortable than it had out in the woods. He tucked the blanket snug around it with a tenderness that surprised himself. He wondered what he had that it might eat, and even if he knew, how he'd manage feeding it, for it seemed to have no mouth.

"But you don't need to worry none," he told it. "Now that I got you under a roof, you'll be all right. I don't know too much about it, but I'll take care of you the best I can."

By now it was getting on toward evening, and he looked out the window and saw that the cows he had been hunting had come home by themselves.

"I got to go get the milking done and the other chores," he told the thing lying on the bed, "but it won't take me long. I'll be right back."

Old Mose loaded up the stove so the kitchen would stay warm and he tucked the thing in once again, then got his milk pails and went down to the barn.

He fed the sheep and pigs and horses and he milked the cows. He hunted eggs and shut the chicken house. He pumped a tank of water.

Then he went back to the house.

It was dark now and he lit the oil lamp on the table, for he was against electricity. He'd refused to sign up when REA had run out the line and a lot of the neighbors had gotten sore at him for being uncooperative. Not that he cared, of course.

He had a look at the thing upon the bed. It didn't seem to be any better, or any worse, for that matter. If it had been a sick lamb or an ailing calf, he could have known right off how it was getting on, but this thing was different. There was no way to tell.

He fixed himself some supper and ate it and wished he knew how to feed the thing. And he wished, too, that he knew how to help it. He'd got it under shelter and he had it warm, but was that right or wrong for something like this? He had no idea.

He wondered if he should try to get some help, then felt squeamish about asking help when he couldn't say exactly what had to be helped. But then he wondered how he would feel himself if he were in a far, strange country, all played out and sick, and no one to get him any help because they didn't know exactly what he was.

That made up his mind for him and he walked over to the phone. But should he call a doctor or a veterinarian?

He decided to call the doctor because the thing was in the house. If it had been in the barn, he would have called the veterinarian.

He was on a rural line and the hearing wasn't good and he was halfway deaf, so he didn't use the phone too often. He had told himself at times it was nothing but another aggravation and there had been a dozen times he had threatened to have it taken out. But now he was glad he hadn't.

The operator got old Doctor Benson and they couldn't hear one another too well, but Mose finally made the doctor understand who was calling and that he needed him and the doctor said he'd come.

With some relief, Mose hung up the phone and was just standing there, not doing anything, when he was struck by the thought that there might be others of these things down there in the woods. He had no idea what they were or what they might be doing or where they might be going, but it was pretty evident that the one upon the bed was some sort of stranger from a very distant place. It stood to reason that there might be more than one of them, for far traveling was a lonely business and anyone—or anything—would like to have some company along.

He got the lantern down off the peg and lit it and went stumping out the door. The night was as black as a stack of cats and the lantern light was feeble, but that made not a bit of difference, for Mose knew this farm of his like the back of his hand.

He went down the path into the woods. It was a spooky place, but it took more than woods at night to spook Old Mose. At the place where he had found the thing, he looked around, pushing through the brush and holding the lantern high so he could see a bigger area, but he didn't find another one of them.

He did find something else, though—a sort of outsize birdcage made of metal lattice work that had wrapped itself around an eight-inch hickory tree. He tried to pull it loose, but it was jammed so tight that he couldn't budge it.

He sighted back the way it must have come. He could see where it had plowed its way through the upper branches of the trees, and out beyond were stars, shining bleakly with the look of far away.

Mose had no doubt that the thing lying on his bed beside the kitchen stove had come in this birdcage contraption. He marveled some at that, but he didn't fret himself too much, for the whole thing was so unearthly that he knew he had little chance of pondering it out.

He walked back to the house and he scarcely had the lantern blown out and hung back on its peg than he heard a car drive up.

The doctor, when he came up to the door, became a little grumpy at seeing Old Mose standing there.

"You don't look sick to me," the doctor said. "Not sick enough to drag me clear out here at night."

"I ain't sick," said Mose.

"Well, then," said the doctor, more grumpily than ever, "what did you mean by phoning me?"

"I got someone who is sick," said Mose. "I hope you can help him. I would have tried myself, but I don't know how to go about it."

The doctor came inside and Mose shut the door behind him.

"You got something rotten in here?" asked the doctor.

"No, it's just the way he smells. It was pretty bad at first, but I'm getting used to it by now."

The doctor saw the thing lying on the bed and went over to it. Old Mose heard him sort of gasp and could see him standing there, very stiff and straight. Then he bent down and had a good look at the critter on the bed.

When he straightened up and turned around to Mose, the only thing that kept him from being downright angry was that he was so flabbergasted.

"Mose," he yelled, "what *is* this?"

"I don't know," said Mose. "I found it in the woods and it was hurt and wailing and I couldn't leave it there."

"You think it's sick?"

"I know it is," said Mose. "It needs help awful bad. I'm afraid it's dying."

The doctor turned back to the bed again and pulled the blanket down, then went and got the lamp so that he could see. He looked the critter up and down, and he prodded it with a skittish finger, and he made the kind of mysterious clucking sound that only doctors make.

Then he pulled the blanket back over it again and took the lamp back to the table.

"Mose," he said, "I can't do a thing for it."

"But you're a doctor!"

"A human doctor, Mose. I don't know what this thing is, but it isn't human. I couldn't even guess what is wrong with it, if anything. And I wouldn't know what could be safely done for it even if I could diagnose its illness. I'm not even sure it's an animal. There are a lot of things about it that argue it's a plant."

Then the doctor asked Mose straight out how he came to find it and Mose told him exactly how it happened. But he didn't tell him anything about the birdcage, for when he thought about it, it sounded so fantastic that he couldn't bring himself to tell it. Just finding the critter and having it here was bad enough, without throwing in the birdcage.

"I tell you what," the doctor said. "You got something here that's outside all human knowledge. I doubt there's ever been a thing like this seen on Earth before. I have no idea what it is and I wouldn't try to guess. If I were you, I'd get in touch with the university up at Madison. There might be someone there who could get it figured out. Even if they couldn't they'd be interested. They'd want to study it."

Mose went to the cupboard and got the cigar box almost full of silver dollars and paid the doctor. The doctor put the dollars in his pocket, joshing Mose about his eccentricity.

But Mose was stubborn about his silver dollars. "Paper money don't seem legal, somehow," he declared. "I like the feel of silver and the way it clinks. It's got authority."

The doctor left and he didn't seem as upset as Mose had been afraid he might be. As soon as he was gone, Mose pulled up a chair and sat down beside the bed.

It wasn't right, he thought, that the thing should be so sick and no one to help—no one who knew any way to help it.

He sat in the chair and listened to the ticking of the clock, loud in the kitchen silence, and the crackling of the wood burning in the stove.

Looking at the thing lying on the bed, he had an almost fierce hope that it could get well again and stay with him. Now that its birdcage was all banged up, maybe there'd be nothing it could do but stay. And he hoped it would, for already the house felt less lonely.

Sitting in the chair between the stove and bed, Mose realized how lonely it had been. It had not been quite so bad until Towser died. He had tried to bring himself to get another dog, but he never had been able to. For there was no dog that would take the place of Towser and it had seemed unfaithful to even try. He could have gotten a cat, of course, but that would remind him too much of Molly; she had been very fond of cats, and until the time she died, there had always been two or three of them underfoot around the place.

But now he was alone. Alone with his farm and his stubbornness and his silver dollars. The doctor thought, like all the rest of them, that the only silver Mose had was in the cigar box in the cupboard. There wasn't one of them who knew about the old iron kettle piled plumb full of them, hidden underneath the floorboards of the living room. He chuckled at the thought of how he had them fooled. He'd give a lot to see his neighbors' faces if they could only know. But he was not the one to tell them. If they were to find it out, they'd have to find it out themselves.

He nodded in the chair and finally he slept, sitting upright, with his chin resting on his chest and his crossed arms wrapped around himself as if to keep him warm.

When he woke, in the dark before the dawn, with the lamp flickering on the table and the fire in the stove burned low, the alien had died.

There was no doubt of death. The thing was cold and rigid and the husk that was its body was rough and drying out—as a corn stalk in the field dries out, whipping in the wind once the growing had been ended.

Mose pulled the blanket up to cover it, and although this was early to do the chores, he went out by lantern light and got them done.

After breakfast, he heated water and washed his face and shaved, and it was the first time in years he'd shaved any day but Sunday. Then he put on his one good suit and slicked down his hair and got the old jalopy out of the machine shed and drove into town.

He hunted up Eb Dennison, the town clerk, who also was the secretary of the cemetery association.

"Eb," he said, "I want to buy a lot."

"But you've got a lot," protested Eb.

"That plot," said Mose, "is a family plot. There's just room for me and Molly."

"Well, then," asked Eb, "why another one? You have no other members of the family."

"I found someone in the woods," said Mose. "I took him home and he died last night. I plan to bury him."

"If you found a dead man in the woods," Eb warned him, "you better notify the coroner and sheriff."

"In time I may," said Mose, not intending to. "Now how about that plot?"

Washing his hands of the affair entirely, Eb sold him the plot.

Having bought his plot, Mose went to the undertaking establishment run by Albert Jones.

"Al," he said, "there's been a death out at the house. A stranger I found out in the woods. He doesn't seem to have anyone and I aim to take care of it."

"You got a death certificate?" asked Al, who subscribed to none of the niceties affected by most funeral parlor operators.

"Well, no, I haven't."

"Was there a doctor in attendance?"

"Doc Benson came out last night."

"He should have made you out one. I'll give him a ring."

He phoned Doctor Benson and talked with him a while and got red around the gills. He finally slammed down the phone and turned on Mose.

"I don't know what you're trying to pull off," he fumed, "but Doc tells me this thing of yours isn't even human. I don't take care of dogs or cats or—"

"This ain't no dog or cat."

"I don't care what it is. It's got to be human for me to handle it. And don't go trying to bury it in the cemetery, because it's against the law."

Considerably discouraged, Mose left the undertaking parlor and trudged slowly up the hill toward the town's one and only church.

He found the minister in his study working on a sermon. Mose sat down in a chair and bumbled his battered hat around and around in his work-scarred hands.

"Parson," he said, "I'll tell you the story from first to last," and he did. He added, "I don't know what it is. I guess no one else does, either. But it's dead and in need of decent burial and that's the least that I can do. I can't bury it in the cemetery, so I suppose I'll have to find a place for it on the farm. I wonder if you could bring yourself to come out and say a word or two."

The minister gave the matter some deep consideration.

"I'm sorry, Mose," he said at last. "I don't believe I can. I am not sure at all the church would approve of it."

"This thing may not be human," said Old Mose, "but it is one of God's critters."

The minister thought some more, and did some wondering out loud, but made up his mind finally that he couldn't do it.

So Mose went down the street to where his car was waiting and drove home, thinking about what heels some humans are.

Back at the farm again, he got a pick and shovel and went into the garden, and there, in one corner of it, he dug a grave. He went out to the machine shed to hunt up some boards to make the thing a casket, but it turned out that he had used the last of the lumber to patch up the hog pen.

Mose went to the house and dug around in a chest in one of the back rooms which had not been used for years, hunting for a sheet to use as a winding shroud, since there would be no casket. He couldn't find a sheet, but he did unearth an old white linen tablecloth. He figured that would do, so he took it to the kitchen.

He pulled back the blanket and looked at the critter lying there in death and a sort of lump came into his throat at the thought of it—how it had died so lonely and so far from home without a creature of its own to spend its final hours with. And naked, too, without a stitch of clothing and with no possession, with not a thing to leave behind as a remembrance of itself.

He spread the tablecloth out on the floor beside the bed and lifted the thing and laid it on the tablecloth. As he laid it down, he saw the pocket in it—if it was a pocket—a sort of slitted flap in the center of what could be its chest. He ran his hand across the pocket area. There was a lump inside it. He crouched for a long moment beside the body, wondering what to do.

Finally he reached his fingers into the flap and took out the thing that bulged. It was a ball, a little bigger than a tennis ball, made of cloudy glass—or, at least, it looked like glass. He squatted there, staring at it, then took it to the window for a better look.

There was nothing strange at all about the ball. It was just a cloudy ball of glass and it had a rough, dead feel about it, just as the body had.

He shook his head and took it back and put it where he'd found it and wrapped the body securely in the cloth. He carried it to the garden and put it in the grave. Standing solemnly at the head of the grave, he said a few short words and then shoveled in the dirt.

He had meant to make a mound above the grave and he had intended to put up a cross, but at the last he didn't do either one of these. There would be snoopers. The word would get around and they'd be coming out and hunting for the spot where he had buried this thing he had found out in the woods. So there must be no mound to mark the place and no cross as well. Perhaps it was for the best, he told himself, for what could he have carved or written on the cross?

By this time it was well past noon and he was getting hungry, but he didn't stop to eat, because there were other things to do. He went out into the pasture and caught up Bess and hitched her to the stoneboat and went down into the woods.

He hitched her to the birdcage that was wrapped around the tree and she pulled it loose as pretty as you please. Then he loaded it on the stoneboat and hauled it up the hill and stowed it in the back of the machine shed, in the far corner by the forge.

After that, he hitched Bess to the garden plow and gave the garden a cultivating that it didn't need so it would be fresh dirt all over and no one could locate where he'd dug the grave.

He was just finishing the plowing when Sheriff Doyle

drove up and got out of the car. The sheriff was a soft-spoken man, but he was no dawdler. He got right to the point.

"I hear," he said, "you found something in the woods."

"That I did," said Mose.

"I hear it died on you."

"Sheriff, you heard right."

"I'd like to see it, Mose."

"Can't. I buried it. And I ain't telling where."

"Mose," the sheriff said, "I don't want to make you trouble, but you did an illegal thing. You can't go finding people in the woods and just bury them when they up and die on you."

"You talk to Doc Benson?"

The sheriff nodded. "He said it wasn't any kind of thing he'd ever seen before. He said it wasn't human."

"Well, then," said Mose, "I guess that lets you out. If it wasn't human, there could be no crime against property. There's been no one around to claim they owned the thing, is there?"

The sheriff rubbed his chin. "No, there hasn't. Maybe you're right. Where did you study law?"

"I never studied law. I never studied nothing. I just use common sense."

"Doc said something about the folks up at the university might want a look at it."

"I tell you, Sheriff," said Mose. "This thing came here from somewhere and it died. I don't know where it came from and I don't know what it was and I don't hanker none to know. To me it was just a living thing that needed help real bad. It was alive and it had its dignity and in death it commanded some respect. When the rest of you refused it decent burial, I did the best I could. And that is all there is to it."

"All right, Mose," the sheriff said, "if that's how you want it."

He turned around and stalked back to the car. Mose

stood beside old Bess hitched to her plow and watched him drive away. He drove fast and reckless as if he might be angry.

Mose put the plow away and turned the horse back to the pasture and by now it was time to do chores again.

He got the chores all finished and made himself some supper and after supper sat beside the stove, listening to the ticking of the clock, loud in the silent house, and the crackle of the fire.

All night long the house was lonely.

The next afternoon, as he was plowing corn, a reporter came and walked up the row with him and talked with him when he came to the end of the row. Mose didn't like this reporter much. He was too flip and he asked some funny questions, so Mose clammed up and didn't tell him much.

A few days later, a man showed up from the university and showed him the story the reporter had gone back and written. The story made fun of Mose.

"I'm sorry," the professor said. "These newspapermen are unaccountable. I wouldn't worry too much about anything they write."

"I don't," Mose told him.

The man from the university asked a lot of questions and made quite a point about how important it was that he should see the body.

But Mose only shook his head. "It's at peace," he said. "I aim to leave it that way."

The man went away disgusted, but still quite dignified.

For several days there were people driving by and dropping in, the idly curious, and there were some nieghbors Mose hadn't seen for months. But he gave them all short shrift and in a little while they left him alone and he went on with his farming and the house stayed lonely.

He thought again that maybe he should get a dog, but he thought of Towser and he couldn't do it.

One day, working in the garden, he found the plant that grew out of the grave. It was a funny-looking plant and his first impulse was to root it out.

But he didn't do it, for the plant intrigued him. It was a kind he'd never seen before and he decided he would let it grow, for a while at least, to see what kind it was. It was a bulky, fleshy plant, with heavy, dark-green, curling leaves, and it reminded him in some ways of the skunk cabbage that burgeoned in the woods come spring.

There was another visitor, the queerest of the lot. He was a dark and intense man who said he was the president of a flying saucer club. He wanted to know if Mose had talked with the thing he'd found out in the woods and seemed terribly disappointed when Mose told him he hadn't. He wanted to know if Mose had found a vehicle the creature might have traveled in and Mose lied to him about it. He was afraid, the wild way the man was acting, that he might demand to search the place, and if he had, he'd likely have found the birdcage hidden in the machine shed back in the corner by the forge. But the man got to lecturing Mose about withholding vital information.

Finally Mose had taken all he could of it, so he stepped into the house and picked up the shotgun from behind the door. The president of the flying saucer club said good-by rather hastily and got out of there.

Farm life went on as usual, with the corn laid by and the haying started and out in the garden the strange plant kept on growing and now was taking shape. Old Mose couldn't believe his eyes when he saw the sort of shape it took and he spent long evening hours just standing in the garden, watching it and wondering if his loneliness were playing tricks on him.

The morning came when he found the plant standing at the door and waiting for him. He should have been surprised, of course, but he really wasn't, for he had lived with it, watching it of eventide, and although he had not dared admit it even to himself, he had known what it was.

For here was the creature he'd found in the woods, no longer sick and keening, no longer close to death, but full of life and youth.

It was not the same entirely, though. He stood and looked at it and could see the differences—the little differences that might have been those between youth and age, or between a father and a son, or again the differences expressed in an evolutionary pattern.

"Good morning," said Mose, not feeling strange at all to be talking to the thing. "It's good to have you back."

The thing standing in the yard did not answer him. But that was not important; he had not expected that it would. The one important point was that he had something he could talk to.

"I'm going out to do the chores," said Mose. "You want to tag along?"

It tagged along with him and it watched him as he did the chores and he talked to it, which was a vast improvement over talking to himself.

At breakfast, he laid an extra plate for it and pulled up an extra chair, but it turned out the critter was not equipped to use a chair, for it wasn't hinged to sit.

Nor did it eat. That bothered Mose at first, for he was hospitable, but he told himself that a big, strong, strapping youngster like this one knew enough to take care of itself, and he probably didn't need to worry too much about how it got along.

After breakfast, he went out to the garden, with the critter accompanying him, and sure enough, the plant was gone. There was a collapsed husk lying on the ground, the outer covering that had been the cradle of the creature at his side.

Then he went to the machine shed and the creature saw the birdcage and rushed over to it and looked it over minutely. Then it turned around to Mose and made a sort of pleading gesture.

Mose went over to it and laid his hands on one of the twisted bars and the critter stood beside him and laid its hands on, too, and they pulled together. It was no use. They could move the metal some, but not enough to pull it back in shape again.

They stood and looked at one another, although looking may not be the word, for the critter had no eyes to look with. It made some funny motions with its hands, but Mose couldn't understand. Then it lay down on the floor and showed him how the birdcage ribs were fastened to the base.

It took a while for Mose to understand how the fastening worked and he never did know exactly why it did. There wasn't, actually, any reason that it should work that way.

First you applied some pressure, just the right amount at the exact and correct angle, and the bar would move a little. Then you applied some more pressure, again the exact amount and at the proper angle, and the bar would move some more. You did this three times and the bar came loose, although there was, God knows, no reason why it should.

Mose started a fire in the forge and shoveled in some coal and worked the bellows while the critter watched. But when he picked up the bar to put it in the fire, the critter got between him and the forge and wouldn't let him near. Mose realized then he couldn't—or wasn't supposed to—heat the bar to straighten it and he never questioned the entire rightness of it. For, he told himself, this thing must surely know the proper way to do it.

So he took the bar over to the anvil and started hammering it back into shape again, cold, without the use of fire, while the critter tried to show him the shape that it should be. It took quite a while, but finally it was straightened out to the critter's satisfaction.

Mose figured they'd have themselves a time getting the bar back in place again, but it slipped on as slick as could be.

Then they took off another bar and this one went faster now that Mose had the hang of it.

But it was hard and grueling labor. They worked all day and only straightened out five bars.

It took four solid days to get the bars on the birdcage hammered into shape and all the time the hay was waiting to be cut.

But it was all right with Mose. He had someone to talk to and the house had lost its loneliness.

When they got the bars back in place, the critter slipped into the cage and started fooling with a dingus on the roof of it that looked like a complicated basket. Mose, watching, figured that the basket was some sort of control.

The critter was discouraged. It walked around the shed looking for something and seemed unable to find it. It came back to Mose and made its despairing, pleading gesture. Mose showed it iron and steel; he dug into a carton where he kept bolts and clamps and bushings and scraps of metal and other odds and ends, finding brass and copper and even some aluminum, but it wasn't any of these.

And Mose was glad—a bit ashamed for feeling glad, but glad all the same.

For it had been clear to him that when the birdcage was all ready, the critter would be leaving him. It had been impossible for Mose to stand in the way of the repair of the cage, or to refuse to help. But now that it apparently couldn't be, he found himself well pleased.

Now the critter would have to stay with him and he'd have someone to talk to and the house would not be lonely. It would be welcome, he told himself, to have folks again. The critter was almost as good a companion as Towser.

Next morning, while Mose was fixing breakfast, he reached up in the cupboard to get the box of oatmeal and his hand struck the cigar box and it came crashing to the floor. It fell over on its side and the lid came open and the dollars went free-wheeling all around the kitchen.

Out of the corner of his eye, Mose saw the critter leaping quickly in pursuit of one of them. It snatched it up and turned to Mose, with the coin held between its fingers, and a sort of thrumming noise was coming out of the nest of worms on top of it.

It bent and scooped up more of them and cuddled them and danced a sort of jig, and Mose knew, with a sinking heart, that it had been silver the critter had been hunting.

So Mose got down on his hands and knees and helped the critter gather up all the dollars. They put them back into the cigar box and Mose picked up the box and gave it to the critter.

The critter took it and hefted it and had a disappointed look. Taking the box over to the table, it took the dollars out and stacked them in neat piles and Mose could see it was very disappointed.

Perhaps, after all, Mose thought, it had not been silver the thing had been hunting for. Maybe it had made a mistake in thinking that the silver was some other kind of metal.

Mose got down the oatmeal and poured it into some water and put it on the stove. When it was cooked and the coffee was ready, he carried his breakfast to the table and sat down to eat.

The critter still was standing across the table from him, stacking and restacking the piles of silver dollars. And now it showed him with a hand held above the stacks, that it needed more of them. This many stacks, it showed him, and each stack so high.

Mose sat stricken, with a spoon full of oatmeal halfway to his mouth. He thought of all those other dollars, the iron kettle packed with them, underneath the floorboards in the living room. And he couldn't do it; they were the only thing he had—except the critter now. And he could not give them up so the critter could go and leave him too.

He ate his bowl of oatmeal without tasting it and drank two cups of coffee. And all the time the critter stood there and showed him how much more it needed.

"I can't do it for you," Old Mose said. "I've done all you can expect of any living being. I found you in the woods and I gave you warmth and shelter. I tried to help you, and when I couldn't, at least I gave you a place to die in. I buried you and protected you from all those other people and I did not pull you up when you started growing once again. Surely you can't expect me to keep on giving endlessly."

But it was no good. The critter could not hear him and he did not convince himself.

He got up from the table and walked into the living room with the critter trailing him. He loosened the floorboards and took out the kettle, and the critter, when it saw what was in the kettle, put its arms around itself and hugged in happiness.

They lugged the money out to the machine shed and Mose built a fire in the forge and put the kettle in the fire and started melting down that hard-saved money.

There were times he thought he couldn't finish the job, but he did.

The critter got the basket out of the birdcage and put it down beside the forge and dipped out the molten silver with an iron ladle and poured it here and there into the basket, shaping it in place with careful hammer taps.

It took a long time, for it was exacting work, but finally it was done and the silver almost gone. The critter lugged the basket back into the birdcage and fastened it in place.

It was almost evening now and Mose had to go and do the chores. He half expected the thing might haul out the birdcage and be gone when he came back to the house. And he tried to be sore at it for its selfishness—it had taken from him and had not tried to pay him back—it had not, so far as he could tell, even tried to thank him. But he made a poor job of being sore at it.

It was waiting for him when he came from the barn carrying two pails full of milk. It followed him inside the house and stood around and he tried to talk to it. But he didn't have the heart to do much talking. He could not forget that it would be leaving, and the pleasure of its present company was lost in his terror of the loneliness to come.

For now he didn't even have his money to help ward off the loneliness.

As he lay in bed that night, strange thoughts came creeping in upon him—the thought of an even greater loneliness than he had ever known upon this runty farm, the terrible, devastating loneliness of the empty wastes that lay between the stars, a driven loneliness while one hunted for a place or person that remained a misty thought one could not define, but which it was most important one should find.

It was a strange thing for him to be thinking, and quite suddenly he knew it was no thought of his, but of this other that was in the room with him.

He tried to raise himself, he fought to raise himself, but he couldn't do it. He held his head up a moment, then fell back upon the pillow and went sound asleep.

Next morning, after Mose had eaten breakfast, the two of them went to the machine shed and dragged the birdcage out. It stood there, a weird alien thing, in the chill brightness of the dawn.

The critter walked up to it and started to slide between two of the bars, but when it was halfway through, it stepped out again and moved over to confront Old Mose.

"Good-by, friend," said Mose. "I'll miss you."

There was a strange stinging in his eyes.

The other held out its hand in farewell, and Mose took it and there was something in the hand he grasped, something round and smooth that was transferred from its hand to his.

The thing took its hand away and stepped quickly to the birdcage and slid between the bars. The hands reached for the basket and there was a sudden flicker and the birdcage was no longer there.

Mose stood lonely in the barnyard, looking at the place where there was no birdcage and remembering what he had felt or thought—or been told?—the night before as he lay in bed.

Already the critter would be there, out between the stars, in that black and utter loneliness, hunting for a place or thing or person that no human mind could grasp.

Slowly Mose turned around to go back to the house, to get the pails and go down to the barn to get the milking done.

He remembered the object in his hand and lifted his still-clenched fist in front of him. He opened his fingers and the little crystal ball lay there in his palm—and it was exactly like the one he'd found in the slitted flap in the body he had buried in the garden. Except that one had been dead and cloudy and this one had the living glow of a distant-burning fire.

Looking at it, he had the strange feeling of a happiness and comfort such as he had seldom known before, as if there were many people with him and all of them were friends.

He closed his hand upon it and the happiness stayed on—and it was all wrong, for there was not a single reason that he should be happy. The critter finally had left him and his money was all gone and he had no friends, but still he kept on feeling good.

He put the ball into his pocket and stepped spryly for the house to get the milking pails. He pursed up his whiskered lips and began to whistle and it had been a long, long time since he had even thought to whistle.

Maybe he was happy, he told himself, because the critter had not left without stopping to take his hand and try to say good-by.

And a gift, no matter how worthless it might be, how cheap a trinket, still had a basic value in simple sentiment. It had been many years since anyone had bothered to give him a gift.

It was dark and lonely and unending in the depths of space with no Companion. It might be long before another was obtainable.

It perhaps was a foolish thing to do, but the old creature had been such a kind savage, so fumbling and so pitiful and eager to help. And one who travels far and fast must likewise travel light. There had been nothing else to give.

The Big Front Yard

Hiram Taine came awake and sat up in his bed.

Towser was barking and scratching at the floor.

"Shut up," Taine told the dog.

Towser cocked quizzical ears at him and then resumed the barking and scratching at the floor.

Taine rubbed his eyes. He ran a hand through his rat's-nest head of hair. He considered lying down again and pulling up the covers.

But not with Towser barking.

"What's the matter with you, anyhow?" he asked Towser, with not a little wrath.

"*Whuff*," said Towser, industriously proceeding with his scratching at the floor.

"If you want out," said Taine, "all you got to do is open the screen door. You know how it is done. You do it all the time."

Towser quieted his barking and sat down heavily, watching his master getting out of bed.

Taine put on his shirt and pulled on his trousers, but didn't bother with his shoes.

Towser ambled over to a corner, put his nose down to the baseboard and snuffled moistly.

"You got a mouse?" asked Taine.

"*Whuff*," said Towser, most emphatically.

"I can't ever remember you making such a row about a mouse," Taine said, slightly puzzled. "You must be off your rocker."

It was a beautiful summer morning. Sunlight was pouring through the open window.

Good day for fishing, Taine told himself, then remembered that there'd be no fishing, for he had to go out and look up that old four-poster maple bed that he had heard about up Woodman way. More than likely, he thought, they'd want twice as much as it was worth. It was getting so, he told himself, that a man couldn't make an honest dollar. Everyone was getting smart about antiques. He got up off the bed and headed for the living room.

"Come on," he said to Towser.

Towser came along, pausing now and then to snuffle into corners and to whuffle at the floor.

"You got it bad," said Taine.

Maybe it's a rat, he thought. The house was getting old.

He opened the screen door and Towser went outside.

"Leave that woodchuck be today," Taine advised him. "It's a losing battle. You'll never dig him out."

Towser went around the corner of the house.

Taine noticed that something had happened to the sign that hung on the post beside the driveway. One of the chains had become unhooked and the sign was dangling.

He padded out across the driveway slab and the grass, still wet with dew, to fix the sign. There was nothing wrong with it—just the unhooked chain. Might have been the wind, he thought, or some passing urchin. Although probably not an urchin. He got along with kids. They never bothered him, like they did some others in the village. Banker Stevens, for example. They were always pestering Stevens.

He stood back a way to be sure the sign was straight.

It read, in big letters:

HANDY MAN

And under that, in smaller lettering:

I fix anything

And under that:

ANTIQUES FOR SALE

What have you got to trade?

Maybe, he told himself, he'd ought to have two signs, one for his fix-it shop and one for antiques and trading. Some day, when he had the time, he thought, he'd paint a couple of new ones. One for each side of the driveway. It would look neat that way.

He turned around and looked across the road at Turner's Woods. It was a pretty sight, he thought. A sizable piece of woods like that right at the edge of town. It was a place for birds and rabbits and woodchucks and squirrels and it was full of forts built through generations by the boys of Willow Bend.

Some day, of course, some smart operator would buy it up and start a housing development or something equally objectionable and when that happened a big slice of his own boyhood would be cut out of his life.

Towser came around the corner of the house. He was sidling along, sniffing at the lowest row of siding and his ears were cocked with interest.

"That dog is nuts," said Taine and went inside.

He went into the kitchen, his bare feet slapping on the floor.

He filled the teakettle, set it on the stove and turned the burner on underneath the kettle.

He turned on the radio, forgetting that it was out of kilter.

When it didn't make a sound, he remembered and, disgusted, snapped it off. That was the way it went, he thought. He fixed other people's stuff, but never got around to fixing any of his own.

He went into the bedroom and put on his shoes. He threw the bed together.

Back in the kitchen the stove had failed to work again. The burner beneath the kettle still was cold.

Taine hauled off and kicked the stove. He lifted the kettle and held his palm above the burner. In a few seconds he could detect some heat.

"Worked again," he told himself.

Some day, he knew, kicking the stove would fail to work. When that happened, he'd have to get to work on it. Probably wasn't more than a loose connection.

He put the kettle back onto the stove.

There was a clatter out in front and Taine went out to see what was going on.

Beasly, the Hortons' yardboy-chauffeur-gardener-et cetera was backing a rickety old truck up the driveway. Beside him sat Abbie Horton, the wife of H. Henry Horton, the village's most important citizen. In the back of the truck, lashed on with ropes and half-protected by a garish red and purple quilt, stood a mammoth television set. Taine recognized it from of old. It was a good ten years out of date and still, by any standard, it was the most expensive set ever to grace any home in Willow Bend.

Abbie hopped out of the truck. She was an energetic, bustling, bossy woman.

"Good morning, Hiram," she said. "Can you fix this set again?"

"Never saw anything that I couldn't fix," said Taine, but nevertheless he eyed the set with something like dismay. It was not the first time he had tangled with it and he knew what was ahead.

"It might cost you more than it's worth," he warned her. "What you really need is a new one. This set is getting old and—"

"That's just what Henry said," Abbie told him, tartly. "Henry wants to get one of the color sets. But I won't part with this one. It's not just TV, you know. It's a combination with radio and a record player and the wood and style are just right for the other furniture, and besides—"

"Yes, I know," said Taine, who'd heard it all before.

Poor old Henry, he thought. What a life the man must lead. Up at that computer plant all day long, shooting off his face and bossing everyone, then coming home to a life of petty tyranny.

"Beasly," said Abbie, in her best drill-sergeant voice, "you get right up there and get that thing untied."

"Yes'm," Beasly said. He was a gangling, loose-jointed man who didn't look too bright.

"And see you be careful with it. I don't want it all scratched up."

"Yes'm," said Beasly.

"I'll help," Taine offered.

The two climbed into the truck and began unlashing the old monstrosity.

"It's heavy," Abbie warned. "You two be careful of it."

"Yes'm," said Beasly.

It was heavy and it was an awkward thing to boot, but Beasly and Taine horsed it around to the back of the house and up the stoop and through the back door and down the basement stairs, with Abbie following eagle-eyed behind them, alert to the slightest scratch.

The basement was Taine's combination workshop and display room for antiques. One end of it was filled with benches and with tools and machinery and boxes full of odds and ends and piles of just plain junk were scattered everywhere. The other end housed a collection of rickety chairs, sagging bedposts, ancient highboys, equally ancient lowboys, old coal scuttles painted gold, heavy iron fireplace screens and a lot of other stuff that he had collected from far and wide for as little as he could possibly pay for it.

He and Beasly set the TV down carefully on the floor. Abbie watched them narrowly from the stairs.

"Why, Hiram," she said, excited, "you put a ceiling in the basement. It looks a whole lot better."

"Huh?" asked Taine.

"The ceiling. I said you put in a ceiling."

Taine jerked his head up and what she said was true. There was a ceiling there, but he'd never put it in.

He gulped a little and lowered his head, then jerked it quickly up and had another look. The ceiling was still there.

"It's not that block stuff," said Abbie with open admiration. "You can't see any joints at all. How did you manage it?"

Taine gulped again and got back his voice. "Something I thought up," he told her weakly.

"You'll have to come over and do it to our basement. Our basement is a sight. Beasly put the ceiling in the amusement room, but Beasly is all thumbs."

"Yes'm," Beasly said contritely.

"When I get the time," Taine promised, ready to promise anything to get them out of there.

"You'd have a lot more time," Abbie told him acidly, "if you weren't gadding around all over the country buying up that broken-down old furniture that you call antiques. Maybe you can fool the city folks when they come driving out here, but you can't fool me."

"I make a lot of money out of some of it," Taine told her calmly.

"And lose your shirt on the rest of it," she said.

"I got some old china that is just the kind of stuff you

are looking for," said Taine. "Picked it up just a day or two ago. Made a good buy on it. I can let you have it cheap."

"I'm not interested," she said and clamped her mouth tight shut.

She turned around and went back up the stairs.

"She's on the prod today," Beasly said to Taine. "It will be a bad day. It always is when she starts early in the morning."

"Don't pay attention to her," Taine advised.

"I try not to, but it ain't possible. You sure you don't need a man? I'd work for you cheap."

"Sorry, Beasly. Tell you what—come over some night soon and we'll play some checkers."

"I'll do that, Hiram. You're the only one who ever asks me over. All the others ever do is laugh at me or shout."

Abbie's voice came bellowing down the stairs. "Beasly, are you coming? Don't go standing there all day. I have rugs to beat."

"Yes'm," said Beasly, starting up the stairs.

At the truck, Abbie turned on Taine with determination: "You'll get that set fixed right away? I'm lost without it."

"Immediately," said Taine.

He stood and watched them off, then looked around for Towser, but the dog had disappeared. More than likely he was at the woodchuck hole again, in the woods across the road. Gone off, thought Taine, without his breakfast, too.

The teakettle was boiling furiously when Taine got back to the kitchen. He put coffee in the maker and poured in the water. Then he went downstairs.

The ceiling was still there.

He turned on all the lights and walked around the basement, staring up at it.

It was a dazzling white material and it appeared to be translucent—up to a point, that is. One could see into it, but he could not see through it. And there were no signs of seams. It was fitted neatly and tightly around the water pipes and the ceiling lights.

Taine stood on a chair and rapped his knuckles against it sharply. It gave out a bell-like sound, almost exactly as if he'd rapped a fingernail against a thinly-blown goblet.

He got down off the chair and stood there, shaking his head. The whole thing was beyond him. He had spent part of the evening repairing Banker Stevens' lawn mower and there'd been no ceiling then.

He rummaged in a box and found a drill. He dug out one of the smaller bits and fitted it in the drill. He plugged in the cord and climbed on the chair again and tried the bit against the ceiling. The whirling steel slid wildly back and forth. It didn't make a scratch. He switched off the drill and looked closely at the ceiling. There was not a mark upon it. He tried again, pressing against the drill with all his strength. The bit went *ping* and the broken end flew across the basement and hit the wall.

Taine stepped down off the chair. He found another bit and fitted it in the drill and went slowly up the stairs, trying to think. But he was too confused to think. That ceiling should not be up there, but there it was. And unless he went stark, staring crazy and forgetful as well, he had not put it there.

In the living room, he folded back one corner of the worn and faded carpeting and plugged in the drill. He knelt and started drilling in the floor. The bit went smoothly through the old oak flooring, then stopped. He put on more pressure and the drill spun without getting any bite.

And there wasn't supposed to be anything underneath that wood! Nothing to stop a drill. Once through the flooring, it should have dropped into the space between the joists.

Taine disengaged the drill and laid it to one side.

He went into the kitchen and the coffee now was ready. But before he poured it, he pawed through a cabinet drawer and found a pencil flashlight. Back in the living room he shone the light into the hole that the drill had made.

There was something shiny at the bottom of the hole.

He went back to the kitchen and found some day-old doughnuts and poured a cup of coffee. He sat at the kitchen table, eating doughnuts and wondering what to do.

There didn't appear, for the moment at least, much that he could do. He could putter around all day trying to figure out what had happened to his basement and probably not be any wiser than he was right now.

His money-making Yankee soul rebelled against such a horrid waste of time.

There was, he told himself, that maple four-poster that he should be getting to before some unprincipled city antique dealer should run afoul of it. A piece like that, he figured, if a man had any luck at all, should sell at a right good price. He might turn a handsome profit on it if he only worked it right.

Maybe, he thought, he could turn a trade on it. There was the table model TV set that he had traded a pair of ice skates for last winter. Those folks out Woodman way might conceivably be happy to trade the bed for a reconditioned TV set, almost like brand new. After all, they probably weren't using the bed and, he hoped fervently, had no idea of the value of it.

He ate the doughnuts hurriedly and gulped down an extra cup of coffee. He fixed a plate of scraps for Towser and set it outside the door. Then he went down into the basement and got the table TV and put it in the pickup truck. As an afterthought, he added a reconditioned shotgun which would be perfectly all right if a man were careful not to use these far-reaching, powerful shells, and a few other odds and ends that might come in handy on a trade.

He got back late, for it had been a busy and quite satisfactory day. Not only did he have the four-poster loaded on the truck, but he had as well a rocking chair, a fire screen, a bundle of ancient magazines, an old-fashioned barrel churn, a walnut highboy and a Governor Winthrop on which some half-baked, slaphappy decorator had applied a coat of apple-green paint. The television set, the shotgun and five dollars had gone into the trade. And what was better yet, he'd managed it so well that the Woodman family probably was dying of laughter at this very moment about how they'd taken him.

He felt a little ashamed of it—they'd been such friendly people. They had treated him so kindly and had him stay for dinner and had sat and talked with him and shown him about the farm and even asked him to stop by if he went through that way again.

He'd wasted the entire day, he thought, and he rather hated that, but maybe it had been worth it to build up his reputation out that way as the sort of character who had softening of the head and didn't know the value of a dollar. That way, maybe some other day, he could do some more business in the neighborhood.

He heard the television set as he opened the back door, sounding loud and clear, and he went clattering down the basement stairs in something close to a panic. For now that he'd traded off the table model, Abbie's set was the only one downstairs and Abbie's set was broken.

It was Abbie's set, all right. It stood just where he and Beasly had put it down that morning and there was nothing wrong with it—nothing wrong at all. It was even televising color.

Televising color!

He stopped at the bottom of the stairs and leaned against the railing for support.

The set kept right on televising color.

Taine stalked the set and walked around behind it.

The back of the cabinet was off, leaning against a bench that stood behind the set, and he could see the innards of it glowing cheerily.

He squatted on the basement floor and squinted at the lighted innards and they seemed a good deal different from the way that they should be. He'd repaired the set many times before and he thought he had a good idea of what the working parts would look like. And now they all seemed different, although just how he couldn't tell.

A heavy step sounded on the stairs and a hearty voice came booming down to him.

"Well, Hiram, I see you got it fixed."

Taine jackknifed upright and stood there slightly frozen and completely speechless.

Henry Horton stood foursquarely and happily on the stairs, looking very pleased.

"I told Abbie that you wouldn't have it done, but she said for me to come over anyway—hey, Hiram, it's in color! How did you do it, man?"

Taine grinned sickly. "I just got fiddling around," he said.

Henry came down the rest of the stairs with a stately step and stood before the set, with his hands behind his back, staring at it fixedly in his best executive manner.

He slowly shook his head. "I never would have thought," he said, "that it was possible."

"Abbie mentioned that you wanted color."

"Well, sure. Of course I did. But not on this old set. I never would have expected to get color on this set. How did you do it, Hiram?"

Taine told the solemn truth. "I can't rightly say," he said.

Henry found a nail keg standing in front of one of the benches and rolled it out in front of the old-fashioned set. He sat down warily and relaxed into solid comfort.

"That's the way it goes," he said. "There are men like

you, but not very many of them. Just Yankee tinkerers. You keep messing around with things, trying one thing here and another there and before you know it you come up with something."

He sat on the nail keg, staring at the set.

"It's sure a pretty thing," he said. "It's better than the color they have in Minneapolis. I dropped in at a couple of the places the last time I was there and looked at the color sets. And I tell you honest, Hiram, there wasn't one of them that was as good as this."

Taine wiped his brow with his shirt sleeve. Somehow or other, the basement seemed to be getting warm. He was fine sweat all over.

Henry found a big cigar in one of his pockets and held it out to Taine.

"No, thanks. I never smoke."

"Perhaps you're wise," said Henry. "It's a nasty habit."

He stuck the cigar into his mouth and rolled it east to west.

"Each man to his own," he proclaimed expansively. "When it comes to a thing like this, you're the man to do it. You seem to think in mechanical contraptions and electronic circuits. Me, I don't know a thing about it. Even in the computer game, I still don't know a thing about it; I hire men who do. I can't even saw a board or drive a nail. But I can organize. You remember, Hiram, how everybody snickered when I started up the plant?"

"Well, I guess some of them did, at that."

"You're darn tooting they did. They went around for weeks with their hands up to their faces to hide smart-aleck grins. They said, what does Henry think he's doing, starting up a computer factory out here in the sticks; he doesn't think he can compete with those big companies in the east, does he? And they didn't stop their grinning until I sold a couple of dozen units and had orders for a year or two ahead."

He fished a lighter from his pocket and lit the cigar

carefully, never taking his eyes off the television set.

"You got something there," he said, judiciously, "that may be worth a mint of money. Some simple adaptation that will fit on any set. If you can get color on this old wreck, you can get color on any set that's made."

He chuckled moistly around the mouthful of cigar. "If RCA knew what was happening here this minute, they'd go out and cut their throats."

"But I don't know what I did," protested Taine.

"Well, that's all right," said Henry, happily. "I'll take this set up to the plant tomorrow and turn loose some of the boys on it. They'll find out what you have here before they're through with it."

He took the cigar out of his mouth and studied it intently, then popped it back in again.

"As I was saying, Hiram, that's the difference in us. You can do the stuff, but you miss the possibilities. I can't do a thing, but I can organize it once the thing is done. Before we get through with this, you'll be wading in twenty-dollar bills clear up to your knees."

"But I don't have—"

"Don't worry. Just leave it all to me. I've got the plant and whatever money we may need. We'll figure out a split."

"That's fine of you," said Taine mechanically.

"Not at all," Henry insisted, grandly. "It's just my aggressive, grasping sense of profit. I should be ashamed of myself, cutting in on this."

He sat on the keg, smoking and watching the TV perform in exquisite color.

"You know, Hiram," he said, "I've often thought of this, but never got around to doing anything about it. I've got an old computer up at the plant that we will have to junk because it's taking up room that we really need. It's one of our early models, a sort of experimental job that went completely sour. It sure is a screwy thing. No one's ever been able to make much out of it. We tried some approaches that probably were wrong—or maybe they were right, but we didn't know enough to make them quite come off. It's been standing in a corner all these years and I should have junked it long ago. But I sort of hate to do it. I wonder if you might not like it—just to tinker with."

"Well, I don't know," said Taine.

Henry assumed an expansive air. "No obligation, mind you. You may not be able to do a thing with it—I'd frankly be surprised if you could, but there's no harm in trying. Maybe you'll decide to tear it down for the salvage you can get. There are several thousand dollars' worth of equipment in it. Probably you could use most of it one way or another."

"It might be interesting," conceded Taine, but not too enthusiastically.

"Good," said Henry, with an enthusiasm that made up for Taine's lack of it. "I'll have the boys cart it over tomorrow. It's a heavy thing. I'll send along plenty of help to get it unloaded and down into the basement and set up."

Henry stood up carefully and brushed cigar ashes off his lap.

"I'll have the boys pick up the TV set at the same time," he said. "I'll have to tell Abbie you haven't got it fixed yet. If I ever let it get into the house, the way it's working now, she'd hold onto it."

Henry climbed the stairs heavily and Taine saw him out the door into the summer night.

Taine stood in the shadow, watching Henry's shadowed figure go across the Widow Taylor's yard to the next street behind his house. He took a deep breath of the fresh night air and shook his head to try to clear his buzzing brain, but the buzzing went right on.

Too much had happened, he told himself. Too much for any single day—first the ceiling and now the TV set.

Once he had a good night's sleep he might be in some sort of shape to try to wrestle with it.

Towser came around the corner of the house and limped slowly up the steps to stand beside his master. He was mud up to his ears.

"You had a day of it, I see," said Taine. "And, just like I told you, you didn't get the woodchuck."

"*Woof*," said Towser, sadly.

"You're just like a lot of the rest of us," Taine told him, severely. "Like me and Henry Horton and all the rest of us. You're chasing something and you think you know what you're chasing, but you really don't. And what's even worse, you have no faint idea of why you're chasing it."

Towser thumped a tired tail upon the stoop.

Taine opened the door and stood to one side to let Towser in, then went in himself.

He went through the refrigerator and found part of a roast, a slice or two of luncheon meat, a dried-out slab of cheese and half a bowl of cooked spaghetti. He made a pot of coffee and shared the food with Towser.

Then Taine went back downstairs and shut off the television set. He found a trouble lamp and plugged it in and poked the light into the innards of the set.

He squatted on the floor, holding the lamp, trying to puzzle out what had been done to the set. It was different, of course, but it was a little hard to figure out in just what ways it was different. Someone had tinkered with the tubes and had them twisted out of shape and there were little white cubes of metal tucked here and there in what seemed to be an entirely haphazard and illogical manner—although, Taine admitted to himself, there probably was no haphazardness. And the circuit, he saw, had been rewired and a good deal of wiring had been added.

But the most puzzling thing about it was that the whole thing seemed to be just jury-rigged—as if someone had done no more than a hurried, patch-up job to get the set back in working order on an emergency and temporary basis.

Someone, he thought!

And who had that someone been?

He hunched around and peered into the dark corners of the basement and he felt innumerable and many-legged imaginary insects running on his body.

Someone had taken the back off the cabinet and leaned it against the bench and had left the screws which held the back laid neatly in a row upon the floor. Then they had jury-rigged the set and jury-rigged it far better than it had ever been before.

If this was a jury-job, he wondered, just what kind of job would it have been if they had had the time to do it up in style?

They hadn't had the time, of course. Maybe they had been scared off when he had come home—scared off even before they could get the back on the set again.

He stood up and moved stiffly away.

First the ceiling in the morning—and now, in the evening, Abbie's television set.

And the ceiling, come to think of it, was not a ceiling only. Another liner, if that was the proper term for it, of the same material as the ceiling, had been laid beneath the floor, forming a sort of boxed-in area between the joists. He had struck that liner when he had tried to drill into the floor.

And what, he asked himself, if all the house were like that, too?

There was just one answer to it all: *There was something in the house with him!*

Towser had heard that *something* or smelled it or in some other manner sensed it and had dug frantically at the floor in an attempt to dig it out, as if it were a woodchuck.

Except that this, whatever it might be, certainly was

no woodchuck.

He put away the trouble light and went upstairs.

Towser was curled up on a rug in the living room beside the easy chair and beat his tail in polite decorum in greeting to his master.

Taine stood and stared down at the dog. Towser looked back at him with satisfied and sleepy eyes, then heaved a doggish sigh and settled down to sleep.

Whatever Towser might have heard or smelled or sensed this morning, it was quite evident that as of this moment he was aware of it no longer.

Then Taine remembered something else.

He had filled the kettle to make water for the coffee and had set it on the stove. He had turned on the burner and it had worked the first time.

He hadn't had to kick the stove to get the burner going.

He woke in the morning and someone was holding down his feet and he sat up quickly to see what was going on.

But there was nothing to be alarmed about; it was only Towser who had crawled into bed with him and now lay sprawled across his feet.

Towser whined softly and his back legs twitched as he chased dream rabbits.

Taine eased his feet from beneath the dog and sat up, reaching for his clothes. It was early, but he remembered suddenly that he had left all of the furniture he had picked up the day before out there in the truck and should be getting downstairs where he could start reconditioning it.

Towser went on sleeping.

Taine stumbled to the kitchen and looked out of the window and there, squatted on the back stoop, was Beasly, the Horton man-of-all-work.

Taine went to the back door to see what was going on.

"I quit them, Hiram," Beasly told him. "She kept on pecking at me every minute of the day and I couldn't do a thing to please her, so I up and quit."

"Well, come on in," said Taine. "I suppose you'd like a bite to eat and a cup of coffee."

"I was kind of wondering if I could stay here, Hiram. Just for my keep until I can find something else."

"Let's have breakfast first," said Taine, "then we can talk about it."

He didn't like it, he told himself. He didn't like it at all. In another hour or so Abbie would show up and start stirring up a ruckus about how he'd lured Beasly off. Because, no matter how dumb Beasly might be, he did a lot of work and took a lot of nagging and there wasn't anyone else in town who would work for Abbie Horton.

"Your ma used to give me cookies all the time," said Beasly. "Your ma was a real good woman, Hiram."

"Yes, she was," said Taine.

"My ma used to say that you folks were quality, not like the rest in town, no matter what kind of airs they were always putting on. She said your family was among the first settlers. Is that really true, Hiram?"

"Well, not exactly first settlers, I guess, but this house has stood here for almost a hundred years. My father used to say there never was a night during all those years that there wasn't at least one Taine beneath its roof. Things like that, it seems, meant a lot to father."

"It must be nice," said Beasly, wistfully, "to have a feeling like that. You must be proud of this house, Hiram."

"Not really proud; more like belonging. I can't imagine living in any other house."

Taine turned on the burner and filled the kettle. Carrying the kettle back, he kicked the stove. But there wasn't any need to kick it; the burner was already beginning to take on a rosy glow.

Twice in a row, Taine thought. This thing is getting better!

"Gee, Hiram," said Beasly, "this is a dandy radio."

"It's no good," said Taine. "It's broke. Haven't had the time to fix it."

"I don't think so, Hiram. I just turned it on. It's beginning to warm up."

"It's beginning to—Hey, let me see!" yelled Taine.

Beasly told the truth. A faint hum was coming from the tubes.

A voice came in, gaining in volume as the set warmed up.

It was speaking gibberish.

"What kind of talk is that?" asked Beasly.

"I don't know," said Taine, close to panic now.

First the television set, then the stove and now the radio!

He spun the tuning knob and the point crawled slowly across the dial face instead of spinning across as he remembered it, and station after station sputtered and went past.

He tuned in the next station that came up and it was strange lingo, too—and he knew by then exactly what he had.

Instead of a $39.50 job, he had here on the kitchen table an all-band receiver like they advertised in the fancy magazines.

He straightened up and said to Beasly: "See if you can get someone speaking English. I'll get on with the eggs."

He turned on the second burner and got out the frying pan. He put it on the stove and found eggs and bacon in the refrigerator.

Beasly got a station that had band music playing.

"How's that?" he asked.

"That's fine," said Taine.

Towser came out from the bedroom, stretching and yawning. He went to the door and showed he wanted out.

Taine let him out.

"If I were you," he told the dog, "I'd lay off that woodchuck. You'll have all the woods dug up."

"He ain't digging after any woodchuck, Hiram."

"Well, a rabbit, then."

"Not a rabbit, either. I snuck off yesterday when I was supposed to be beating rugs. That's what Abbie got so sore about."

Taine grunted, breaking eggs into the skillet.

"I snuck away and went over to where Towser was. I talked with him and he told me it wasn't a woodchuck or a rabbit. He said it was something else. I pitched in and helped him dig. Looks to me like he found an old tank of some sort buried out there in the woods."

"Towser wouldn't dig up any tank," protested Taine. "He wouldn't care about anything except a rabbit or a woodchuck."

"He was working hard," insisted Beasly. "He seemed to be excited."

"Maybe the woodchuck just dug his hold under this old tank or whatever it might be."

"Maybe so," Beasly agreed. He fiddled with the radio some more. He got a disk jockey who was pretty terrible.

Taine shoveled eggs and bacon onto plates and brought them to the table. He poured big cups of coffee and began buttering the toast.

"Dive in," he said to Beasly.

"This is good of you, Hiram, to take me in like this. I won't stay no longer than it takes to find a job."

"Well, I didn't exactly say—"

"There are times," said Beasly, "when I get to thinking I haven't got a friend and then I remember your ma, how nice she was to me and all—"

"Oh, all right," said Taine.

He knew when he was licked.

He brought the toast and a jar of jam to the table and sat down, beginning to eat.

"Maybe you got something I could help you with," suggested Beasly, using the back of his hand to wipe egg off his chin.

"I have a load of furniture out in the driveway. I could use a man to help me get it down into the basement."

"I'll be glad to do that," said Beasly. "I am good and strong. I don't mind work at all. I just don't like people jawing at me."

They finished breakfast and then carried the furniture down into the basement. They had some trouble with the Governor Winthrop, for it was an unwieldy thing to handle.

When they finally horsed it down, Taine stood off and looked at it. The man, he told himself, who slapped paint onto that beautiful cherrywood had a lot to answer for.

He said to Beasly: "We have to get the paint off that thing there. And we must do it carefully. Use paint remover and a rag wrapped around a spatula and just sort of roll it off. Would you like to try it?"

"Sure, I would. Say, Hiram, what will we have for lunch?"

"I don't know," said Taine. "We'll throw something together. Don't tell me you're hungry."

"Well, it was sort of hard work, getting all that stuff down here."

"There are cookies in the jar on the kitchen shelf," said Taine. "Go and help yourself."

When Beasly went upstairs, Taine walked slowly around the basement. The ceiling, he saw, was still intact. Nothing else seemed to be disturbed.

Maybe that television set and the stove and radio, he thought, was just their way of paying rent to me. And if that were the case, he told himself, whoever they might be, he'd be more than willing to let them stay right on.

He looked around some more and could find nothing wrong.

He went upstairs and called to Beasly in the kitchen.

"Come on out to the garage, where I keep the paint. We'll hunt up some remover and show you how to use it."

Beasly, a supply of cookies clutched in his hand,

trotted willingly behind him.

As they rounded the corner of the house they could hear Towser's muffled barking. Listening to him, it seemed to Taine that he was getting hoarse.

Three days, he thought—or was it four?

"If we don't do something about it," he said, "that fool dog is going to get himself worn out."

He went into the garage and came back with two shovels and a pick.

"Come on," he said on Beasly. "We have to put a stop to this before we have any peace."

Towser had done himself a noble job of excavation. He was almost completely out of sight. Only the end of his considerably bedraggled tail showed out of the hole he had clawed in the forest floor.

Beasly had been right about the tank like thing. One edge of it showed out of one side of the hole.

Towser backed out of the hole and sat down heavily, his whiskers dripping clay, his tongue hanging out of the side of his mouth.

"He says that it's about time that we showed up," said Beasly.

Taine walked around the hole and knelt down. He reached down a hand to brush the dirt off the projecting edge of Beasly's tank. The clay was stubborn and hard to wipe away, but from the feel of it the tank was heavy metal.

Taine picked up a shovel and rapped it against the tank. The tank gave out a clang.

They got to work, shoveling away a foot or so of topsoil that lay above the object. It was hard work and the thing was bigger than they had thought and it took some time to get it uncovered, even roughly.

"I'm hungry," Beasly complained.

Taine glanced at his watch. It was almost one o'clock.

"Run on back to the house," he said to Beasly. "You'll

find something in the refrigerator and there's milk to drink."

"How about you, Hiram? Ain't you ever hungry?"

"You could bring me back a sandwich and see if you can find a trowel."

"What you want a trowel for?"

"I want to scrape the dirt off this thing and see what it is."

He squatted down beside the thing they had unearthed and watched Beasly disappear into the woods.

"Towser," he said, "this is the strangest animal you ever put to ground."

A man, he told himself, might better joke about it—if to do no more than keep his fear away.

Beasly wasn't scared, of course. Beasly didn't have the sense to be scared of a thing like this.

Twelve feet wide by twenty long and oval shaped. About the size, he thought, of a good-size living room. And there never had been a tank of that shape or size in all of Willow Bend.

He fished his jackknife out of his pocket and started to scratch away the dirt at one point on the surface of the thing. He got a square inch of free dirt and it was no metal such as he had ever seen. It looked for all the world like glass.

He kept on scraping at the dirt until he had a clean place as big as an outstretched hand.

It wasn't any metal. He'd almost swear to that. It looked like cloudy glass—like the milk-glass goblets and bowls he was always on the lookout for. There were a lot of people who were plain nuts about it and they'd pay fancy prices for it.

He closed the knife and put it back into his pocket and squatted, looking at the oval shape that Towser had discovered.

And the conviction grew: Whatever it was that had come to live with him undoubtedly had arrived in this same contraption. From space or time, he thought, and was astonished that he thought it, for he'd never thought such a thing before.

He picked up his shovel and began to dig again, digging down this time, following the curving side of this alien thing that lay within the earth.

And as he dug, he wondered. What should he say about this—or should he say anything? Maybe the smartest course would be to cover it again and never breathe a word about it to a living soul.

Beasly would talk about it, naturally. But no one in the village would pay attention to anything that Beasly said. Everyone in Willow Bend knew Beasly was cracked.

Beasly finally came back. He carried three inexpertly-made sandwiches wrapped in an old newspaper and a quart bottle almost full of milk.

"You certainly took your time," said Taine, slightly irritated.

"I got interested," Beasly explained.

"Interested in what?"

"Well, there were three big trucks and they were lugging a lot of heavy stuff down into the basement. Two or three big cabinets and a lot of other junk. And you know Abbie's television set? Well, they took the set away. I told them that they shouldn't, but they took it anyway."

"I forgot," said Taine. "Henry said he'd send the computer over and I plumb forgot."

Taine ate the sandwiches, sharing them with Towser, who was very grateful in a muddy way.

Finished, Taine rose and picked up his shovel.

"Let's get to work," he said.

"But you got all that stuff down in the basement."

"That can wait," said Taine. "This job we have to finish."

It was getting dusk by the time they finished.

Taine leaned wearily on his shovel.

Twelve feet by twenty across the top and ten feet

deep—and all of it, every bit of it, made of the milk-glass stuff that sounded like a bell when you whacked it with a shovel.

They'd have to be small, he thought, if there were many of them, to live in a space that size, especially if they had to stay there very long. And that fitted in, of course, for if they weren't small they couldn't now be living in the space between the basement joists.

If they were really living there, thought Taine. If it wasn't all just a lot of supposition.

Maybe, he thought, even if they had been living in the house, they might be there no longer—for Towser had smelled or heard or somehow sensed them in the morning, but by that very night he'd paid them no attention.

Taine slung his shovel across his shoulder and hoisted the pick.

"Come on," he said, "let's go. We've put in a long, hard day."

They tramped out through the brush and reached the road. Fireflies were flickering off and on in the woody darkness and the street lamps were swaying in the summer breeze. The stars were hard and bright.

Maybe they still were in the house, thought Taine. Maybe when they found out that Towser had objected to them, they had fixed it so he'd be aware of them no longer.

They probably were highly adaptive. It stood to good reason they would have to be. It hadn't taken them too long, he told himself grimly, to adapt to a human house.

He and Beasly went up the gravel driveway in the dark to put the tools away in the garage and there was no front on the house and the driveway was cut off abruptly and there was nothing but the curving wall of what apparently had been the end of the garage.

They came up to the curving wall and stopped, squinting unbelieving in the summer dark.

There was no garage, no porch, no front of the house at all. It was as if someone had taken the opposite corners of the front of the house and bent them together until they touched, folding the entire front of the building inside the curvature of the bent-together corners.

Taine now had a curved-front house. Although it was, actually, not as simple as all that, for the curvature was not in proportion to what actually would have happened in case of such a feat. The curve was long and graceful and somehow got quite apparent. It was as if the front of the house had been eliminated and an illusion of the rest of the house had been summoned to mask the disappearance.

Taine dropped the shovel and the pick and they clattered on the driveway gravel. He put his hand up to his face and wiped it across his eyes, as if to clear his eyes of something that could not possibly be there.

And when he took the hand away it had not changed a bit.

There was no front to the house.

Then he was running around the house, hardly knowing he was running, and there was a fear inside of him at what had happened to the house.

But the back of the house was all right. It was exactly as it had always been.

He clattered up the stoop with Beasly and Towser running close behind him. He pushed open the door and burst into the entry and scrambled up the stairs into the kitchen and went across the kitchen in three strides to see what had happened to the front of the house.

At the door between the kitchen and the living room he stopped and his hands went out to grasp the door jamb as he stared in disbelief at the windows of the living room.

It was night outside. There could be no doubt of that. He had seen the fireflies flicking in the brush and weeds and the street lamps had been lit and the stars were out.

But a flood of sunlight was pouring through the

windows of the living room and out beyond the windows lay a land that was not Willow Bend.

"Beasly," he gasped, "look out there in front!"

Beasly looked.

"What place is that?" he asked.

"That's what I'd like to know."

Towser had found his dish and was pushing it around the kitchen floor with his nose, by way of telling Taine that it was time to eat.

Taine went across the living room and opened the front door. The garage, he saw, was there. The pickup stood with its nose against the open garage door and the car was safe inside.

There was nothing wrong with the front of the house at all.

But if the front of the house was all right, that was all that was.

For the driveway was chopped off just a few feet beyond the tail end of the pickup and there was no yard or woods or road. There was just a desert—a flat, far-reaching desert, level as a floor, with occasional boulder piles and haphazard clumps of vegetation and all of the ground covered with sand and pebbles. A big blinding sun hung just above a horizon that seemed much too far away and a funny thing about it was that the sun was in the north, where no proper sun should be. It had a peculiar whiteness, too.

Beasly stepped out on the porch and Taine saw that he was shivering like a frightened dog.

"Maybe," Taine told him, kindly, "you'd better go back in and start making us some supper."

"But, Hiram—"

"It's all right," said Taine. "It's bound to be all right."

"If you say so, Hiram."

He went in and the screen door banged behind him and in a minute Taine heard him in the kitchen.

He didn't blame Beasly for shivering, he admitted to

himself. It was a sort of shock to step out of your front door into an unknown land. A man might eventually get used to it, of course, but it would take some doing.

He stepped down off the porch and walked around the truck and around the garage corner and when he rounded the corner he was half prepared to walk back into familiar Willow Bend—for when he had gone in the back door the village had been there.

There was no Willow Bend. There was more of the desert, a great deal more of it.

He walked around the house and there was no back to the house. The back of the house now was just the same as the front had been before—the same smooth curve pulling the sides of the house together.

He walked on around the house to the front again and there was desert all the way. And the front was still all right. It hadn't changed at all. The truck was there on the chopped-off driveway and the garage was open and the car inside.

Taine walked out a way into the desert and hunkered down and scooped up a handful of the pebbles and the pebbles were just pebbles.

He squatted there and let the pebbles trickle through his fingers.

In Willow Bend there was a back door and there wasn't any front. Here, wherever here might be, there was a front door, but there wasn't any back.

He stood up and tossed the rest of the pebbles away and wiped his dusty hands upon his breeches.

Out of the corner of his eye he caught a sense of movement on the porch and there they were.

A line of tiny animals, if animals they were, came marching down the steps, one behind another. They were four inches high or so and they went on all four feet, although it was plain to see that their front feet were really hands, not feet. They had ratlike faces that were vaguely human, with noses long and pointed. They looked as if they might have scales instead of hide, for their bodies glistened with a rippling motion as they walked. And all of them had tails that looked very much like the coiled-wire tails one finds on certain toys and the tails stuck straight up above them, quivering as they walked.

They came down the steps in single file, in perfect military order, with half a foot or so of spacing between each one of them.

They came down the steps and walked out into the desert in a straight, undeviating line as if they knew exactly where they might be bound. There was something deadly purposeful about them and yet they didn't hurry.

Taine counted sixteen of them and he watched them go out into the desert until they were almost lost to sight.

There go the ones, he thought, who came to live with me. They are the ones who fixed up the ceiling and who repaired Abbie's television set and jiggered up the stove and radio. And more than likely, too, they were the ones who had come to Earth in the strange milk-glass contraption out there in the woods.

And if they had come to Earth in that deal out in the woods, then what sort of place was this?

He climbed the porch and opened the screen door and saw the neat, six-inch circle his departing guests had achieved in the screen to get out of the house. He made a mental note that some day, when he had the time, he would have to fix it.

He went in and slammed the door behind him.

"Beasly," he shouted.

There was no answer.

Towser crawled from beneath the love seat and apologized.

"It's all right, pal," said Taine. "That outfit scared me, too."

He went into the kitchen. The dim ceiling light shone

on the overturned coffee pot, the broken cup in the center of the floor, the upset bowl of eggs. One broken egg was a white and yellow gob on the linoleum.

He stepped down on the landing and saw that the screen door in the back was wrecked beyond repair. Its rusty mesh was broken —exploded might have been a better word—and a part of the frame was smashed.

Taine looked at it in wondering admiration.

"The poor fool," he said. "He went straight through it without opening it at all."

He snapped on the light and went down the basement stairs. Halfway down he stopped in utter wonderment.

To his left was a wall—a wall of the same sort of material as had been used to put in the ceiling.

He stooped and saw that the wall ran clear across the basement, floor to ceiling, shutting off the workshop area.

And inside the workshop, what?

For one thing, he remembered, the computer that Henry had sent over just this morning. Three trucks, Beasly had said—three truckloads of equipment delivered straight into their paws!

Taine sat down weakly on the steps.

They must have thought, he told himself, that he was cooperating! Maybe they had figured that he knew what they were about and so went along with them. Or perhaps they thought he was paying them for fixing up the TV set and the stove and radio.

But to tackle first things first, why had they repaired the TV set and the stove and radio? As a sort of rental payment? As a friendly gesture? Or as a sort of practice run to find out what they could about this world's technology? To find, perhaps, how their technology could be adapted to the materials and conditions on this planet they had found?

Taine raised a hand and rapped with his knuckles on the wall beside the stairs and the smooth white surface gave out a pinging sound.

He laid his ear against the wall and listened closely and it seemed to him he could hear a low-key humming, but if so it was so faint he could not be absolutely sure.

Banker Stevens' lawn mower was in there, behind the wall, and a lot of other stuff waiting for repair. They'd take the hide right off him, he thought, especially Banker Stevens. Stevens was a tight man.

Beasly must have been half-crazed with fear, he thought. When he had seen those things coming up out of the basement, he'd gone clean off his rocker. He'd gone straight through the door without even bothering to try to open it and now he was down in the village yapping to anyone who'd stop to listen to him.

No one ordinarily would pay Beasly much attention, but if he yapped long enough and wild enough, they'd probably do some checking. They'd come storming up here and they'd give the place a going-over and they'd stand goggle-eyed at what they found in front and pretty soon some of them would have worked their way around to sort of running things.

And it was none of their business, Taine stubbornly told himself, his ever-present business sense rising to the fore. There was a lot of real estate lying around out there in his front yard and the only way anyone could get to it was by going through the house. That being the case, it stood to reason that all that land out there was his. Maybe it wasn't any good at all. There might be nothing there. But before he had other people overrunning it, he'd better check and see.

He went up the stairs and out into the garage.

The sun was still just above the northern horizon and there was nothing moving.

He found a hammer and some nails and a few short lengths of plank in the garage and took them in the house.

Towser, he saw, had taken advantage of the situation and was sleeping in the gold-upholstered chair. Taine didn't bother him.

Taine locked the back door and nailed some planks across it. He locked the kitchen and the bedroom windows and nailed planks across them, too.

That would hold the villagers for a while, he told himself, when they came tearing up here to see what was going on.

He got his deer rifle, a box of cartridges, a pair of binoculars and an old canteen out of a closet. He filled the canteen at the kitchen tap and stuffed a sack with food for him and Towser to eat along the way, for there was no time to wait and eat.

Then he went into the living room and dumped Towser out of the gold-upholstered chair.

"Come on, Tows," he said. "We'll go and look things over."

He checked the gasoline in the pickup and the tank was almost full.

He and the dog got in and he put the rifle within easy reach. Then he backed the truck and swung it around and headed out, north, across the desert.

It was easy traveling. The desert was as level as a floor. At times it got a little rough, but no worse than a lot of the back roads he traveled hunting down antiques.

The scenery didn't change. Here and there were low hills, but the desert itself kept on mostly level, unraveling itself into that far-off horizon. Taine kept on driving north, straight into the sun. He hit some sandy stretches, but the sand was firm and hard and he had no trouble.

Half an hour out he caught up with the band of things—all sixteen of them—that had left the house. They were still traveling in line at their steady pace.

Slowing down the truck, Taine traveled parallel with them for a time, but there was no profit in it; they kept on traveling their course, looking neither right or left.

Speeding up, Taine left them behind.

The sun stayed in the north, unmoving, and that certainly was queer. Perhaps, Taine told himself, this world spun on its axis far more slowly than the Earth and the day was longer. From the way the sun appeared to be standing still, perhaps a good deal longer.

Hunched above the wheel, staring out into the endles stretch of desert, the strangeness of it struck him for the first time with its full impact.

This was another world—there could be no doubt of that—another planet circling another star, and where it was in actual space no one on Earth could have the least idea. And yet, through some machination of those sixteen things walking straight in line, it also was lying just outside the front door of his house.

Ahead of him a somewhat larger hill loomed out of the flatness of the desert. As he drew nearer to it, he made out a row of shining objects lined upon its crest. After a time he stopped the truck and got out with the binoculars.

Through the glasses, he saw that the shining things were the same sort of milk-glass contraptions as had been in the woods. He counted eight of them, shining in the sun, perched upon some sort of rock-gray cradles. And there were other cradles empty.

He took the binoculars from his eyes and stood there for a moment, considering the advisability of climbing the hill and investigating closely. But he shook his head. There'd be time for that later on. He'd better keep on moving. This was not a real exploring foray, but a quick reconnaissance.

He climbed into the truck and drove on, keeping watch upon the gas gauge. When it came close to half full he'd have to turn around and go back home again.

Ahead of him he saw a faint whiteness above the dim horizon line and he watched it narrowly. At times it faded away and then came in again, but whatever it might be was so far off he could make nothing of it.

He glanced down at the gas gauge and it was close to the halfway mark. He stopped the pickup and got out with the binoculars.

As he moved around to the front of the machine he was puzzled at how slow and tired his legs were and then remembered—he should have been in bed many hours ago. He looked at his watch and it was two o'clock and that meant, back on Earth, two o'clock in the morning. He had been awake for more than twenty hours and much of that time he had been engaged in the backbreaking work of digging out the strange thing in the woods.

He put up the binoculars and the elusive white line that he had been seeing turned out to be a range of mountains. The great, blue, craggy mass towered up above the desert with the gleam of snow on its peaks and ridges. They were a long way off, for even the powerful glasses brought them in as little more than a misty blueness.

He swept the glasses slowly back and forth and the mountains extended for a long distance above the horizon line.

He brought the glasses down off the mountains and examined the desert that stretched ahead of him. There was more of the same that he had been seeing—the same floor-like levelness, the same occasional mounds, the self-same scraggy vegetation.

And a house!

His hands trembled and he lowered the glasses, then put them up to his face again and had another look. It was a house, all right. A funny-looking house standing at the foot of one of the hillocks, still shadowed by the hillock so that one could not pick it out with the naked eye.

It seemed to be a small house. Its roof was like a blunted cone and it lay tight against the ground, as if it hugged or crouched against the ground. There was an oval opening that probably was a door, but there was no sign of windows.

He took the binoculars down again and stared at the hillock. Four or five miles away, he thought. The gas would stretch that far and even if it didn't he could walk the last few miles into Willow Bend.

It was queer, he thought, that a house should be all alone out here. In all the miles he'd traveled in the desert he'd seen no sign of life beyond the sixteen little ratlike things that marched in single file, no sign of artificial structure other than the eight milk-glass contraptions resting in their cradles.

He climbed into the pickup and put it into gear. Ten minutes later he drew up in front of the house, which still lay within the shadow of the hillock.

He got out of the pickup and hauled his rifle after him. Towser leaped to the ground and stood with his hackles up, a deep growl in his throat.

"What's the matter, boy?" asked Taine.

Towser growled again.

The house stood silent. It seemed to be deserted.

The walls were built, Taine saw, of rude, rough masonry crudely set together, with a crumbling, mudlike substance used in lieu of mortar. The roof originally had been of sod and that was queer, indeed, for there was nothing that came close to sod upon this expanse of desert. But now, although one could see the lines where the sod strips had been fitted together, it was nothing more than earth baked hard by the desert sun.

The house itself was featureless, entirely devoid of any ornament, with no attempt at all to soften the harsh utility of it as a simple shelter. It was the sort of thing that a shepherd people might have put together. It had the look of age about it; the stone had flaked and crumbled in the weather.

Rifle slung beneath his arm, Taine paced toward it. He reached the door and glanced inside and there was darkness and no movement.

He glanced back for Towser and saw that the dog had crawled beneath the truck and was peering out and growling.

"You stick around," said Taine. "Don't go running off."

With the rifle thrust before him, Taine stepped through the door into the darkness. He stood for a long moment to allow his eyes to become accustomed to the gloom.

Finally he could make out the room in which he stood. It was plain and rough, with a rude stone bench along one wall and queer unfunctional niches hollowed in another. One rickety piece of wooden furniture stood in a corner, but Taine could not make out what its use might be.

An old and deserted place, he thought, abandoned long ago. Perhaps a shepherd people might have lived here in some long-gone age, when the desert had been rich and grassy plain.

There was a door into another room and as he stepped through it he heard the faint, far-off booming sound and something else as well—the sound of pouring rain! From the open door that led out through the back he caught a whiff of salty breeze and he stood there frozen in the center of that second room.

Another one!

Another house that led to another world!

He walked slowly forward, drawn toward the outer door, and he stepped out into a cloudy, darkling day with the rain streaming down from wildly racing clouds. Half a mile away, across a field of jumbled, broken, iron-gray boulders, lay a pounding sea that raged upon the coast, throwing great spumes of angry spray high into the air.

He walked out from the door and looked up at the sky, and the raindrops pounded at his face with a stinging fury. There was a chill and a dampness in the air and the place was eldritch—a world jerked straight from some ancient Gothic tale of goblin and of sprite.

He glanced around and there was nothing he could see, for the rain blotted out the world beyond this stretch of coast, but behind the rain he could sense or seemed to sense a presence that sent shivers down his spine.

Gulping in fright, Taine turned around and stumbled back again through the door into the house.

One world away, he thought, was far enough; two worlds away was more than one could take. He trembled at the sense of utter loneliness that tumbled in his skull and suddenly this long-forsaken house became unbearable and he dashed out of it.

Outside the sun was bright and there was welcome warmth. His clothes were damp from rain and little beads of moisture lay on the rifle barrel.

He looked around for Towser and there was no sign of the dog. He was not underneath the pickup; he was nowhere in sight.

Taine called and there was no answer. His voice sounded lone and hollow in the emptiness and silence.

He walked around the house, looking for the dog, and there was no back door to the house. The rough rock walls of the sides of the house pulled in with that funny curvature and there was no back to the house at all.

But Taine was not interested; he had known how it would be. Right now he was looking for his dog and he felt the panic rising in him. Somehow it felt a long way from home.

He spent three hours at it. He went back into the other world again and searched among the tumbled rocks and Towser was not there. He went back to the desert and walked around the hillock and then he climbed to the crest of it and used the binoculars and saw nothing but the lifeless desert, stretching far in all directions.

Dead-beat with weariness, stumbling, half asleep even as he walked, he went back to the pickup.

He leaned against it and tried to pull his wits together.

Continuing as he was would be a useless effort. He had to get some sleep. He had to go back to Willow Bend and fill the tank and get some extra gasoline so that he could range farther afield in his search for Towser.

He couldn't leave the dog out here—that was

unthinkable. But he had to plan, he had to act intelligently. He would be doing Towser no good by stumbling around in his present shape.

He pulled himself into the truck and headed back for Willow Bend, following the occasional faint impressions that his tires had made in the sandy places, fighting a half-dead drowsiness that tried to seal his eyes shut.

Passing the higher hill on which the milk-glass things had stood, he stopped to walk around a bit so he wouldn't fall asleep behind the wheel. And now, he saw, there were only seven of the things resting in their cradles.

But that meant nothing to him now. All that meant anything was to hold off the fatigue that was closing down upon him, to cling to the wheel and wear off the miles, to get back to Willow Bend and get some sleep and then come back again to look for Towser.

Slightly more than halfway home he saw the other car and watched it in numb befuddlement, for this truck that he was driving and the car at home in his garage were the only two vehicles this side of his house.

He pulled the pickup to a halt and tumbled out of it.

The car drew up and Henry Horton and Beasly and a man who wore a star leaped quickly out of it.

"Thank God we found you, man!" cried Henry, striding over to him.

"I wasn't lost," protested Taine. "I was coming back."

"He's all beat out," said the man who wore the star.

"This is Sheriff Hanson," Henry said. "We were following your tracks."

"I lost Towser," Taine mumbled. "I had to go and leave him. Just leave me be and go and hunt for Towser. I can make it home."

He reached out and grabbed the edge of the pickup's door to hold himself erect.

"You broke down the door," he said to Henry. "You broke into my house and you took my car—"

"We had to do it, Hiram. We were afraid that

something might have happened to you. The way that Beasly told it, it stood your hair on end."

"You better get him in the car," the sheriff said. "I'll drive the pickup back."

"But I have to hunt for Towser!"

"You can't do anything until you've had some rest."

Henry grabbed him by the arm and led him to the car and Beasly held the rear door open.

"You got any idea what this place is?" Henry whispered conspiratorially.

"I don't positively know," Taine mumbled. "Might be some other—"

Henry chuckled. "Well, I guess it doesn't really matter. Whatever it may be, it's put us on the map. We're in all the newscasts and the papers are plastering us in headlines and the town is swarming with reporters and cameramen and there are big officials coming. Yes, sir, I tell you, Hiram, this will be the making of us—"

Taine heard no more. He was fast asleep before he hit the seat.

He came awake and lay quietly in the bed and he saw the shades were drawn and the room was cool and peaceful.

It was good, he thought, to wake in a room you knew—in a room that one had known for his entire life, in a house that had been the Taine house for almost a hundred years.

Then memory clouted him and he sat bolt upright.

And now he heard it—the insistent murmur from outside the window.

He vaulted from the bed and pulled one shade aside. Peering out, he saw the cordon of troops that held back the crowd that overflowed his backyard and the backyards back of that.

He let the shade drop back and started hunting for his shoes, for he was fully dressed. Probably Henry and

Beasly, he told himself, had dumped him into bed and pulled off his shoes and let it go at that. But he couldn't remember a single thing of it. He must have gone dead to the world the minute Henry had bundled him into the back seat of the car.

He found the shoes on the floor at the end of the bed and sat down upon the bed to pull them on.

And his mind was racing on what he had to do.

He'd have to get some gasoline somehow and fill up the truck and stash an extra can or two into the back and he'd have to take some food and water and perhaps his sleeping bag. For he wasn't coming back until he found his dog.

He got on his shoes and tied them, then went out into the living room. There was no one there, but there were voices in the kitchen.

He looked out the window and the desert lay outside, unchanged. The sun, he noticed, had climbed higher in the sky, but out in his front yard it was still forenoon.

He looked at his watch and it was six o'clock and from the way the shadows had been falling when he'd peered out of the bedroom window, he knew that it was 6:00 P.M. He realized with a guilty start that he must have slept almost around the clock. He had not meant to sleep that long. He hadn't meant to leave Towser out there that long.

He headed for the kitchen and there were three persons there—Abbie and Henry Horton and a man in military garb.

"There you are," cried Abbie merrily. "We were wondering when you would wake up."

"You have some coffee cooking, Abbie?"

"Yes, a whole pot full of it. And I'll cook up something else for you."

"Just some toast," said Taine. "I haven't got much time. I have to hunt for Towser."

"Hiram," said Henry, "this is Colonel Ryan, National

Guard. He has his boys outside."

"Yes, I saw them through the window."

"Necessary," said Henry. "Absolutely necessary. The sheriff couldn't handle it. The people came rushing in and they'd have torn the place apart. So I called the governor."

"Taine," the colonel said, "sit down. I want to talk with you."

"Certainly," said Taine, taking a chair. "Sorry to be in such a rush, but I lost my dog out there."

"This business," said the colonel, smugly, "is vastly more important than any dog could be."

"Well, Colonel, that just goes to show that you don't know Towser. He's the best dog I ever had and I've had a lot of them. Raised him from a pup and he's been a good friend all these years—"

"All right," the colonel said, "so he is a friend. But still I have to talk with you."

"You just sit and talk," Abbie said to Taine. "I'll fix up some cakes and Henry brought over some of that sausage that we get out on the farm."

The back door opened and Beasly staggered in to the accompaniment of a terrific metallic banging. He was carrying three empty five-gallon gas cans in one hand and two in the other hand and they were bumping and banging together as he moved.

"Say," yelled Taine, "what's going on here?"

"Now, just take it easy," Henry said. "You have no idea the problems that we have. We wanted to get a big gas tank moved through here, but we couldn't do it. We tried to rip out the back of the kitchen to get it through, but we couldn't—"

"You did what!"

"We tried to rip out the back of the kitchen," Henry told him calmly. "You can't get one of those big storage tanks through an ordinary door. But when we tried, we found that the entire house is boarded up inside with the same kind of material that you used down in the basement. You hit it with an axe and it blunts the steel—"

"But, Henry, this is my house and there isn't anyone who has the right to start tearing it apart."

"Fat chance," the colonel said. "What I would like to know, Taine, what is that stuff that we couldn't break through?"

"Now you take it easy, Hiram," cautioned Henry. "We have a big new world waiting for us out there—"

"It isn't waiting for you or anyone," yelled Taine.

"And we have to explore it and to explore it we need a stockpile of gasoline. So since we can't have a storage tank, we're getting together as many gas cans as possible and then we'll run a hose through here—"

"But, Henry—"

"I wish," said Henry sternly, "that you'd quit interrupting me and let me have my say. You can't even imagine the logistics that we face. We're bottlenecked by the size of a regulation door. We have to get supplies out there and we have to get transport. Cars and trucks won't be so bad. We can disassemble them and lug them through piecemeal, but a plane will be a problem."

"You listen to me, Henry. There isn't anyone going to haul a plane through here. This house has been in my family for almost a hundred years and I own it and I have a right to it and you can't come in high-handed and start hauling stuff through it."

"But," said Henry plaintively, "we need a plane real bad. You can cover so much more ground when you have a plane."

Beasly went banging through the kitchen with his cans and out into the living room.

The colonel sighed. "I had hoped, Mr. Taine, that you would understand how the matter stood. To me it seems very plain that it's your patriotic duty to cooperate with us in this. The government, of course, could exercise the right of eminent domain and start condemnation action, but it would rather not do that. I'm speaking unofficially, of course, but I think it's safe to say the government would much prefer to arrive at an amicable agreement."

"I doubt," Taine said, bluffing, not knowing anything about it, "that the right to eminent domain would be applicable. As I understand it, it applies to buildings and to roads—"

"This is a road," the colonel told him flatly. "A road right through your house to another world."

"First," Taine declared, "the government would have to show it was in the public interest and that refusal of the owner to relinquish title amounted to an interference in government procedure and—"

"I think," the colonel said, "that the government can prove it is in the public interest."

"I think," Taine said angrily, "I better get a lawyer."

"If you really mean that," Henry offered, ever helpful, "and you want to get a good one—and I presume you do—I would be pleased to recommend a firm that I am sure would represent your interests most ably and be, at the same time, fairly reasonable in cost."

The colonel stood up, seething. "You'll have a lot to answer, Taine. There'll be a lot of things the government will want to know. First of all, they'll want to know just how you engineered this. Are you ready to tell that?"

"No," said Taine, "I don't believe I am."

And he thought with some alarm: They think that I'm the one who did it and they'll be down on me like a pack of wolves to find out just how I did it. He had visions of the FBI and the State Department and the Pentagon and, even sitting down, he felt shaky in the knees.

The colonel turned around and marched stiffly from the kitchen. He went out the back and slammed the door behind him.

Henry looked at Taine speculatively.

"Do you really mean it?" he demanded. "Do you intend to stand up to them?"

"I'm getting sore," said Taine. "They can't come in here and take over without even asking me. I don't care what anyone may think, this is my house. I was born here and I've lived here all my life and I like the place and—"

"Sure," said Henry. "I know just how you feel."

"I suppose it's childish of me, but I wouldn't mind so much if they showed a willingness to sit down and talk about what they meant to do once they'd taken over. But there seems no disposition to even ask me what I think about it. And I tell you, Henry, this is different than it seems. This isn't a place where we can walk in and take over, no matter what Washington may think. There's something out there and we better watch our step—"

"I was thinking," Henry interrupted, "as I was sitting here, that your attitude is most commendable and deserving of support. It has occurred to me that it would be most unneighborly of me to go on sitting here and leave you in the fight alone. We could hire ourselves a fine array of legal talent and we could fight the case and in the meantime we could form a land and development company and that way we could make sure that this new world of yours is used the way it should be used.

"It stand to reason, Hiram, that I am the one to stand beside you, shoulder to shoulder, in this business since we're already partners in this TV deal."

"What's this about TV?" shrilled Abbie, slapping a plate of cakes down in front of Taine.

"Now, Abbie," Henry said patiently, "I have explained to you already that your TV set is back of that partition down in the basement and there isn't any telling when we can get it out."

"Yes, I know," said Abbie, bringing a platter of sausages and pouring a cup of coffee.

Beasly came in from the living room and went bumbling out the back.

"After all," said Henry, pressing his advantage, "I would

suppose I had some hand in it. I doubt you could have done much without the computer I sent over."

And there it was again, thought Taine. Even Henry thought he'd been the one who did it.

"But didn't Beasly tell you?"

"Beasly said a lot, but you know how Beasly is."

And that was it, of course. To the villagers it would be no more than another Beasly story—another whopper that Beasly had dreamed up. There was no one who believed a word that Beasly said.

Taine picked up the cup and drank his coffee, gaining time to shape an answer and there wasn't any answer. If he told the truth, it would sound far less believable than any lie he'd tell.

"You can tell me, Hiram. After all, we're partners."

He's playing me for a fool, thought Taine. Henry thinks he can play anyone he wants for a fool and sucker.

"You wouldn't believe me if I told you, Henry."

"Well," Henry said, resignedly, getting to his feet, "I guess that part of it can wait."

Beasly came tramping and banging through the kitchen with another load of cans.

"I'll have to have some gasoline," said Taine, "if I'm going out for Towser."

"I'll take care of that right away," Henry promised smoothly. "I'll send Ernie over with his tank wagon and we can run a hose through here and fill up those cans. And I'll see if I can find someone who'll go along with you."

"That's not necessary. I can go alone."

"If we had a radio transmitter. Then you could keep in touch."

"But we haven't any. And, Henry, I can't walk. Towser's out there somewhere—"

"Sure, I know how much you thought of him. You go out and look for him if you think you have to and I'll get started on this other business. I'll get some lawyers lined up and we'll draw up some sort of corporate papers for our land development—"

"And, Hiram," Abbie said, "will you do something for me, please?"

"Why, certainly," said Taine.

"Would you speak to Beasly. It's senseless the way he's acting. There wasn't any call for him to up and leave us. I might have been a little sharp with him, but he's so simple-minded he's infuriating. He ran off and spent half a day helping Towser at digging out that woodchuck and—"

"I'll speak to him," said Taine.

"Thanks, Hiram. He'll listen to you. You're the only one he'll listen to. And I wish you could have fixed my TV set before all this came about. I'm just lost without it. It leaves a hole in the living room. It matched my other furniture, you know."

"Yes I know," said Taine.

"Coming, Abbie?" Henry asked, standing at the door.

He lifted a hand in a confidential farewell to Taine. "I'll see you later, Hiram. I'll get it all fixed up."

I just bet you will, thought Taine.

He went back to the table, after they were gone, and sat down heavily in a chair.

The front door slammed and Beasly came panting in, excited.

"Towser's back!" he yelled. "He's coming back and he's driving in the biggest woodchuck you ever clapped your eyes on."

Taine leaped to his feet.

"Woodchuck! That's an alien planet. It hasn't any woodchucks."

"You come and see," yelled Beasly.

He turned and raced back out again, with Taine following close behind.

It certainly looked considerably like a woodchuck—a sort of man-size woodchuck. More like a woodchuck out of a children's book, perhaps, for it was walking on its hind legs and trying to look dignified even while it kept a weather eye on Towser.

Towser was back a hundred feet or so, keeping a wary distance from the massive chuck. He had the pose of a good sheepherding dog, walking in a crouch, alert to head off any break that the chuck might make.

The chuck came up close to the house and stopped. Then it did an about-face so that it looked back across the desert and it hunkered down.

It swung its massive head to gaze at Beasly and Taine and in the limpid brown eyes Taine saw more than the eyes of an animal.

Taine walked swiftly out and picked up the dog in his arms and hugged him tight against him. Towser twisted his head around and slapped a sloppy tongue across his master's face.

Taine stood with the dog in his arms and looked at the man-size chuck and felt a great relief and an utter thankfulness.

Everything was all right now, he thought. Towser had come back.

He headed for the house and out into the kitchen.

He put Towser down and got a dish and filled it at the tap. He placed it on the floor and Towser lapped at it thirstily, slopping water all over the linoleum.

"Take it easy, there," warned Taine. "You don't want to overdo it."

He hunted in the refrigerator and found some scraps and put them in Towser's dish.

Towser wagged his tail with doggish happiness.

"By rights," said Taine, "I ought to take a rope to you, running off like that."

Beasly came ambling in.

"That chuck is a friendly cuss," he announced. "He's waiting for someone."

"That's nice," said Taine, paying no attention.

He glanced at the clock.

"It's seven-thirty," he said. "We can catch the news. You want to get it Beasly?"

"Sure. I know right where to get it. That fellow from New York."

"That's the one," said Taine.

He walked into the living room and looked out the window. The man-size chuck had not moved. He was sitting with his back to the house, looking back the way he'd come.

Waiting for someone, Beasly had said, and it looked as if he might be, but probably it was all just in Beasly's head.

And if he were waiting for someone, Taine wondered, who might that someone be? *What* might that someone be? Certainly by now the word had spread out there that there was a door into another world. And how many doors, he wondered, had been opened through the ages?

Henry had said that there was a big new world out there waiting for Earthmen to move in. And that wasn't it at all. It was the other way around.

The voice of the news commentator came blasting from the radio in the middle of a sentence:

". . . finally got into the act. Radio Moscow said this evening that the Soviet delegate will make representations in the U.N. tomorrow for the internationalization of this other world and the gateway to it.

"From that gateway itself, the home of a man named Hiram Taine, there is no news. Complete security had been clamped down and a cordon of troops form a solid wall around the house, holding back the crowds. Attempts to telephone the residence are blocked by a curt voice which says that no calls are being accepted for that number. And Taine himself has not stepped from the house."

Taine walked back into the kitchen and sat down.

"He's talking about you," Beasley said importantly.

"Rumor circulated this morning that Taine, a quiet village repairman and dealer in antiques, and until yesterday a relative unknown, had finally returned from a trip which he made out into this new and unknown land. But what he found, if anything, no one yet can say. Nor is there any further information about this other place beyond the fact that it is a desert and, to the moment, lifeless.

"A small flurry of excitement was occasioned late yesterday by the finding of some strange object in the woods across the road from the residence, but this area likewise was swiftly cordoned off and to the moment Colonel Ryan, who commands the troops, will say nothing of what actually was found.

"Mystery man of the entire situation is one Henry Horton, who seems to be the only unofficial person to have entry to the Taine house. Horton, questioned earlier today, had little to say, but managed to suggest an air of great conspiracy. He hinted he and Taine were partners in some mysterious venture and left hanging in midair the half impression that he and Taine had collaborated in opening the new world.

"Horton, it is interesting to note, operates a small computer plant and it is understood on good authority that only recently he delivered a computer to Taine, or at least some sort of machine to which considerable mystery is attached. One story is that this particular machine had been in the process of development for six or seven years.

"Some of the answers to the matter of how all this did happen and what actually did happen must wait upon the findings of a team of scientists who left Washington this evening after an all-day conference at the White House, which was attended by representatives from the military, the State Department, the security division and the special weapons section.

"Throughout the world the impact of what happened

yesterday at Willow Bend can only be compared to the sensation of the news, almost twenty years ago, of the dropping of the first atomic bomb. There is some tendency among many observers to believe that the implications of Willow Bend, in fact, may be even more earthshaking than were those of Hiroshima.

"Washington insists, as is only natural, that this matter is of internal concern only and that it intends to handle the situation as it best affects the national welfare.

"But abroad there is a rising storm of insistence that this is not a matter of national policy concerning one nation, but that it necessarily must be a matter of worldwide concern.

"There is an unconfirmed report that a U.N. observer will arrive in Willow Bend almost momentarily. France, Britain, Bolivia, Mexico and India have already requested permission of Washington to send observers to the scene and other nations undoubtedly plan to file similar requests.

"The world sits on edge tonight, waiting for the word from Willow Bend and—"

Taine reached out and clicked the radio to silence.

"From the sound of it," said Beasly, "we're going to be overrun by a batch of foreigners."

Yes, thought Taine, there might be a batch of foreigners, but not exactly in the sense that Beasly meant. The use of the word, he told himself, so far as any human was concerned, must be outdated now. No man of Earth ever again could be called a foreigner with alien life next door—literally next door. What were the people of the stone house?

And perhaps not the alien life of one planet only, but the alien life of many. For he himself had found another door into yet another planet and there might be many more such doors and what would these other worlds be like, and what was the purpose of the doors?

Someone, *something*, had found a way of going to

another planet short of spanning light-years of lonely space—a simpler and a shorter way than flying through the gulfs of space. And once the way was open, then the way stayed open and it was as easy as walking from one room to another.

But one thing—one ridiculous thing—kept puzzling him and that was the spinning and the movement of the connected planets, of all the planets that must be linked together. You could not, he argued, establish solid, factual links between two objects that move independently of one another.

And yet, a couple of days ago, he would have contended just as stolidly that the whole idea on the face of it was fantastic and impossible. Still it had been done. And once one impossibility was accomplished, what logical man could say with sincerity that the second could not be?

The doorbell rang and he got up to answer it.

It was Ernie, the oil man.

"Henry said you wanted some gas and I came to tell you I can't get it until morning."

"That's all right," said Taine. "I don't need it now."

And swiftly slammed the door.

He leaned against it, thinking: I'll have to face them sometime. I can't keep the door locked against the world. Sometime, soon or late, the Earth and I will have to have this out.

And it was foolish, he thought, for him to think like this, but that was the way it was.

He had something here that the Earth demanded; something that Earth wanted or thought it wanted. And yet, in the last analysis, it was his responsibility. It had happened on his land, it had happened in his house; unwittingly, perhaps, he'd even aided and abetted it.

And the land and house are mine, he fiercely told himself, and that world out there was an extension of his yard. No matter how far or where it went, an extension of his yard.

Beasly had left the kitchen and Taine walked into the living room. Towser had won the right to sleep anywhere he wished.

He walked past the chair to the window and the desert stretched to its far horizon and there before the window sat the man-size woodchuck and Beasly side by side, with their backs turned to the window and staring out across the desert.

Somehow it seemed natural that the chuck and Beasly should be sitting there together—the two of them, it appeared to Taine, might have a lot in common.

And it was a good beginning—that a man and an alien creature from this other world should sit down companionably together.

He tried to envision the setup of these linked worlds, of which Earth was now a part, and the possibilities that lay inherent in the fact of linkage rolled thunder through his brain.

There would be contact between the Earth and these other worlds and what would come of it?

And come to think of it, the contact had been made already, but so naturally, so undramatically, that it failed to register as a great, important meeting. For Beasly and the chuck out there were contact and if it all should go like that, there was absolutely nothing for one to worry over.

This was no haphazard business, he reminded himself. It had been planned and executed with the smoothness of long practice. This was not the first world to be opened and it would not be the last.

The little ratlike things had spanned space—how many light-years of space one could not even guess—in the vehicle which he had unearthed out in the woods. They then had buried it, perhaps as a child might hide a dish by shoving it into a pile of sand. Then they had come to this very house and had set up the apparatus that had made this house a tunnel between one world and another. And once that had been done, the need of crossing space had been canceled out forever. There need be but one crossing and that one crossing would serve to link the planets.

And once the job was done the little ratlike things had left, but not before they had made certain that this gateway to their planet would stand against no matter what assault. They had sheathed the house inside the studdings with a wonder-material that would resist an ax and that, undoubtedly, would resist much more than a simple ax.

And they had marched in drill-order single file out to the hill where eight more of the space machines had rested in their cradles on the hill, and the ratlike things were gone and, perhaps, in time to come, they'd land on another planet and an,other doorway would be opened, a link to yet another world.

But more, Taine thought, than the linking of mere worlds. It would be, as well, the linking of the peoples of those worlds.

The little ratlike creatures were the explorers and the pioneers who sought out other Earthlike planets and the creature waiting with Beasly just outside the window must also serve its purpose and perhaps, in time to come, there would be a purpose which man would also serve.

He turned away from the window and looked around the room and the room was exactly as it had been ever since he could remember it. With all the change outside, with all that was happening outside, the room remained unchanged.

This is the reality, thought Taine, this is all the reality there is. Whatever else may happen, this is where I stand—this room with its fireplace blackened by many winter fires, the bookshelves with the old thumbed volumes, the easy chair, the ancient worn carpet—worn by beloved and unforgotten feet through the many years.

And this also, he knew, was the lull before the storm.

In just a little while the brass would start arriving—the team of scientists, the governmental functionaries, the military, the observers from the other countries, the officials from the U.N.

And against all these, he realized, he stood weaponless and shorn of his strength. No matter what a man might say or think, he could not stand off the world.

This was the last day that this would be the Taine house. After almost a hundred years, it would have another destiny.

And for the first time in all those years there'd be no Taine asleep beneath its roof.

He stood looking at the fireplace and the shelves of books and he sensed the old, pale ghosts walking in the room and he lifted a hesitant hand as if to wave farewell, not only to the ghosts but to the room as well. But before he got it up, he dropped it to his side.

What was the use, he thought.

He went out to the porch and sat down on the steps.

Beasly heard him and turned around.

"He's nice," he said to Taine, patting the chuck upon the back. "He's exactly like a great big teddy bear."

"Yes, I see," said Taine.

"And best of all, I can talk with him."

"Yes, I know," said Taine, remembering that Beasly could talk with Towser, too.

He wondered what it would be like to live in the simple world of Beasly. At times, he decided, it would be comfortable.

The ratlike things had come in the spaceship, but why had they come to Willow Bend, why had they picked this house, the only house in all the village where they would have found the equipment that they needed to build their apparatus so easily and so quickly? For there was no doubt that they had cannibalized the computer to get the equipment they needed. In that, at least, Henry had been right. Thinking back on it, Henry, after all, had played quite a part in it.

Could have they foreseen that on this particular week in this particular house the probability of quickly and easily doing what they had come to do had stood very high?

Did they, with all their other talents and technology, have clairvoyance as well?

"There's someone coming," Beasly said.

"I don't see a thing."

"Neither do I," said Beasly, "but Chuck told me that he saw them."

"Told you!"

"I told you we been talking. There, I can see them too."

They were far off, but they were coming fast—three dots rode rapidly out of the desert.

He sat and watched them come and he thought of going in to get the rifle, but he didn't stir from his seat upon the steps. The rifle would do no good, he told himself. It would be a senseless thing to get it; more than that, a senseless attitude. The least that man could do, he thought, was to meet these creatures of another world with clean and empty hands.

They were closer now and it seemed to him that they were sitting in invisible chairs that traveled very fast.

He saw that they were humanoid, to a degree at least, and there were only three of them.

They came in with a rush and stopped very suddenly a hundred feet or so from where he sat upon the steps.

He didn't move or say a word—there was nothing he could say. It was too ridiculous.

They were, perhaps, a little smaller than himself, and black as the ace of spades, and they wore skintight shorts and vests that were somewhat oversize and both the shorts and vests were the blue of April skies.

But that was not the worst of it.

They sat on saddles, with horns in front and stirrups

and a sort of bedroll tied on the back, but they had no horses.

The saddles floated in the air, with the stirrups about three feet above the ground and the aliens sat easily in the saddles and stared at him and he stared back at them.

Finally he got up and moved forward a step or two and when he did that the three swung from the saddles and moved forward, too, while the saddles hung there in the air, exactly as they'd left them.

Taine walked forward and the three walked forward until they were no more than six feet apart.

"They say hello to you," said Beasly. "They say welcome to you."

"Well, all right, then, tell them—Say, how do you know all this!"

"Chuck tells me what they say and I tell you. You tell me and I tell him and he tells them. That's the way it works. That is what he's here for."

"Well, I'll be—," said Taine. "So you can really talk to him."

"I told you that I could," stormed Beasly. "I told you that I could talk to Towser, too, but you thought that I was crazy."

"Telepathy!" said Taine. And it was worse than ever now. Not only had the ratlike things known all the rest of it, but they'd known of Beasly, too.

"What was that you said, Hiram?"

"Never mind," said Taine. "Tell that friend of yours to tell them I'm glad to meet them and what can I do for them?"

He stood uncomfortably and stared at the three and he saw that their vests had many pockets and that the pockets were crammed, probably with their equivalent of tobacco and handkerchiefs and pocket knives and such.

"They say," said Beasly, "that they want to dicker."

"Dicker?"

"Sure, Hiram. You know, trade."

Beasly chuckled thinly. "Imagine them laying themselves open to a Yankee trader. That's what Henry says you are. He says you can skin a man on the slickest—"

"Leave Henry out of this," snapped Taine. "Let's leave Henry out of something."

He sat down on the ground and the three sat down to face him.

"Ask them what they have in mind to trade."

"Ideas," Beasly said.

"Ideas! That's a crazy thing—"

And then he saw it wasn't.

Of all the commodities that might be exchanged by an alien people, ideas would be the most valuable and the easiest to handle. They'd take no cargo room and they'd upset no economies—not immediately, that is—and they'd make a bigger contribution to the welfare of the cultures than trade in actual goods.

"Ask them," said Taine, "what they'll take for the idea back of those saddles they are riding."

"They say, what have you to offer?"

And that was the stumper. That was the one that would be hard to answer.

Automobiles and trucks, the internal gas engine—well, probably not. Because they already had the saddles. Earth was out of date in transportation from the viewpoint of these people.

Housing architecture—no, that was hardly an idea and, anyhow, there was that other house, so they knew of houses.

Cloth? No, they had cloth.

Paint, he thought. Maybe paint was it.

"See if they are interested in paint," Taine told Beasly.

"They say, what is it? Please explain yourself."

"O.K., then. Let's see. It's a protective device to be spread over almost any surface. Easily packaged and easily applied. Protects against weather and corrosion.

It's decorative, too. Comes in all sorts of colors. And it's cheap to make."

"They shrug in their mind," said Beasly. "They're just slightly interested. But they'll listen more. Go ahead and tell them."

And that was more like it, thought Taine.

That was the kind of language that he could understand.

He settled himself more firmly on the ground and bent forward slightly, flicking his eyes across the three deadpan, ebony faces, trying to make out what they might be thinking.

There was no making out. Those were three of the deadest pans he had ever seen.

It was all familiar. It made him feel at home. He was in his element.

And in the three across from him, he felt somehow subconsciously, he had the best dickering opposition he had ever met. And that made him feel good too.

"Tell them," he said, "that I'm not quite sure. I may have spoken up too hastily. Paint, after all, is a mighty valuable idea."

"They say, just as a favor to them, not that they're really interested, would you tell them a little more."

Got them hooked, Taine told himself. If he could only play it right—

He settled down to dickering in earnest.

Hours later Henry Horton showed up. He was accompanied by a very urbane gentleman, who was faultlessly turned out and who carried beneath his arm an impressive attache case.

Henry and the man stopped on the steps in sheer astonishment.

Taine was squatted on the ground with a length of board and he was daubing paint on it while the aliens watched. From the daubs here and there upon their anatomies, it was plain to see the aliens had been doing some daubing of their own. Spread all over the ground were other lengths of half-painted boards and a couple of dozen old cans of paint.

Taine looked up and saw Henry and the man.

"I was hoping," he said, "that someone would show up."

"Hiram," said Henry, with more importance than usual, "may I present Mr. Lancaster. He is a special representative of the United Nations."

"I'm glad to meet you, sir," said Taine. "I wonder if you would—"

"Mr. Lancaster," Henry explained grandly, "was having some slight difficulty getting through the lines outside, so I volunteered my services. I've already explained to him our joint interest in this matter."

"It was very kind of Mr. Horton," Lancaster said. "There was this stupid sergeant—"

"It's all in knowing," Henry said, "how to handle people."

The remark, Taine noticed, was not appreciated by the man from the U.N.

"May I inquire, Mr. Taine," asked Lancaster, "exactly what you're doing?"

"I'm dickering," said Taine.

"Dickering. What a quaint way of expressing—"

"An old Yankee word," said Henry quickly, "with certain connotations of its own. When you trade with someone you are exchanging goods, but if you're dickering with him you're out to get his hide."

"Interesting," said Lancaster. "And I suppose you're out to skin these gentlemen in the sky-blue vests—"

"Hiram," said Henry, proudly, "is the sharpest dickerer in these parts. He runs an antique business and he has to dicker hard—"

"And may I ask," said Lancaster, ignoring Henry finally, "what you might be doing with these cans of paint? Are these gentlemen potential customers for paint or—"

Taine threw down the board and rose angrily to his feet.

"If you'd both shut up!" he shouted. "I've been trying to say something ever since you got here and I can't get in a word. And I tell you, it's important—"

"Hiram!" Henry exclaimed in horror.

"It's quite all right," said the U.N. man. "We *have* been jabbering. And now, Mr. Taine?"

"I'm backed into a corner," Taine told him, "and I need some help. I've sold these fellows on the idea of paint, but I don't know a thing about it—the principle back of it or how it's made or what goes into it or—"

"But, Mr. Taine, if you're selling them the paint, what difference does it make—"

"I'm not selling them the paint," yelled Taine. "Can't you understand that? They don't want the paint. They want the *idea* of paint, the principle of paint. It's something that they never thought of and they're interested. I offered them the paint idea for the idea of their saddles and I've almost got it—"

"Saddles? You mean those things over there, hanging in the air?"

"That is right. Beasly, would you ask one of our friends to demonstrate a saddle?"

"You bet I will," said Beasly.

"What," demanded Henry, "has Beasly got to do with this?"

"Beasly is an interpreter. I guess you'd call him a telepath. You remember how he always claimed he could talk with Towser?"

"Beasly was always claiming things."

"But this time he was right. He tells Chuck, that funny-looking monster, what I want to say and Chuck tells these aliens. And these aliens tell Chuck and Chuck tells Beasly and Beasly tells me."

"Ridiculous!" snorted Henry. "Beasly hasn't got the sense to be. . . what did you say he was?"

"A telepath," said Taine.

One of the aliens had gotten up and climbed into a saddle. He rode it forth and back. Then he swung out of it and sat down again.

"Remarkable," said the U.N. man. "Some sort of antigravity unit, with complete control. We could make use of that, indeed."

He scraped his hand across his chin.

"And you're going to exchange the idea of paint for the idea of that saddle?"

"That's exactly it," said Taine, "but I need some help. I need a chemist or a paint manufacturer or someone to explain how paint is made. And I need some professor or other who'll understand what they're talking about when they tell me the idea of the saddle."

"I see," said Lancaster. "Yes, indeed, you have a problem. Mr. Taine, you seem to me a man of some discernment—"

"Oh, he's all of that," interrupted Henry. "Hiram's quite astute."

"So I suppose you'll understand," said the U.N. man, "that this whole procedure is quite irregular—"

"But it's not," exploded Taine. "That's the way they operate. They open up a planet and then they exchange ideas. They've been doing that with other planets for a long, long time. And ideas are all they want, just the new ideas, because that is the way to keep on building a technology and culture. And they have a lot of ideas, sir, that the human race can use."

"That is just the point," said Lancaster. "This is perhaps the most important thing that has ever happened to us humans. In just a short year's time we can obtain data and ideas that will put us ahead—theoretically, at least—by a thousand years. And in a thing that is so important, we should have experts on the job—"

"But," protested Henry, "you can't find a man who'll do a better dickering job than Hiram. When you dicker with him your back teeth aren't safe. Why don't you leave him be? He'll do a job for you. You can get your experts and your planning groups together and let Hiram front for you. These folks have accepted him and have proved they'll do business with him and what more do you want? All he needs is a little help."

Beasly came over and faced the U.N. man.

"I won't work with no one else," he said. "If you kick Hiram out of here, then I go with him. Hiram's the only person who ever treated me like a human—"

"There, you see!" Henry said, triumphantly.

"Now, wait a second, Beasly," said the U.N. man. "We could make it worth your while. I should imagine that an interpreter in a situation such as this could command a handsome salary."

"Money don't mean a thing to me," said Beasly. "It won't buy me friends. People still will laugh at me."

"He means it, mister," Henry warned. "There isn't anyone who can be as stubborn as Beasly. I know; he used to work for us."

The U.N. man looked flabbergasted and not a little desperate.

"It will take you quite some time," Henry pointed out, "to find another telepath—leastwise one who can talk to these people here."

The U.N. man looked as if he were strangling. "I doubt," he said, "there's another one on Earth."

"Well, all right," said Beasly, brutally, "let's make up our minds. I ain't standing here all day."

"All right," cried the U.N. man. "You two go ahead. Please, will you go ahead? This is a chance we can't let slip through our fingers. Is there anything you want? Anything I can do for you?"

"Yes, there is," said Taine. "There'll be the boys from Washington and bigwigs from other countries. Just keep them off my back."

"I'll explain most carefully to everyone. There'll be no

interference."

"And I need that chemist and someone who'll know about the saddles. And I need them quick. I can stall these boys a little longer, but not for too much longer."

"Anyone you need," said the U.N. man. "Anyone at all. I'll have them here in hours. And in a day or two there'll be a pool of experts waiting for whenever you may need them—on a moment's notice."

"Sir," said Henry unctuously, "that's most cooperative. Both Hiram and I appreciate it greatly. And now, since this is settled, I understand that there are reporters waiting. They'll be interested in your statement."

The U.N. man, it seemed, didn't have it in him to protest. He and Henry went tramping up the stairs.

Taine turned around and looked out across the desert.

"It's a big front yard," he said.

Good Night, Mr. James

He came alive from nothing. He became aware from unawareness.

He smelled the air of the night and heard the trees whispering on the embankment above him and the breeze that had set the trees to whispering came down to him and felt him over with soft and tender fingers, for all the world as if it were examining him for broken bones or contusions and abrasions.

He sat up and put both his palms down upon the ground beside him to help him sit erect and stared into the darkness. Memory came slowly and when it came it was incomplete and answered nothing.

His name was Henderson James and he was a human being and he was sitting somewhere on a planet that was called the Earth. He was thirty-six years old and he was, in his own way, famous, and comfortably well-off. He lived in an old ancestral home on Summit Avenue, which was a respectable address even if it had lost some of its smartness in the last twenty years or so.

On the road above the slope of the embankment a car went past with its tires whining on the pavement and for a moment its headlight made the treetops glow. Far away, muted by the distance, a whistle cried out. And somewhere else a dog was barking with a flat viciousness.

His name was Henderson James and if that were true, why was he here? Why should Henderson James be sitting on the slope of an embankment, listening to the wind in the trees and to a wailing whistle and a barking dog? Something had gone wrong, some incident that, if he could but remember it, might answer all his questions.

There was a job to do.

He sat and stared into the night and found that he was shivering, although there was no reason why he should, for the night was not that cold. Beyond the embankment he heard the sounds of a city late at night, the distant whine of the speeding car and the far-off wind-broken screaming of a siren. Once a man walked along a street close by and James sat listening to his footsteps until they faded out of hearing.

Something had happened and there was a job to do, a job that he had been doing, a job that somehow had been strangely interrupted by the inexplicable incident which had left him lying here on this embankment.

He checked himself. Clothing. . . shorts and shirt, strong shoes, his wristwatch and the gun in the holster at his side.

A gun?

The job involved a gun.

He had been hunting in the city, hunting something that required a gun. Something that was prowling in the night and a thing that must be killed.

Then he knew the answer, but even as he knew it he sat for a moment wondering at the strange, methodical, step-by-step progression of reasoning that had brought him to the memory. First his name and the basic facts pertaining to himself, then the realization of where he was and the problem of why he happened to be there and finally the realization that he had a gun and that it was meant to be used. It was a logical way to think, a primer schoolbook way to work it out:

I am a man named Henderson James.

I live in a house on Summit Avenue.

Am I in the house on Summit Avenue?

No, I am not in the house on Summit Avenue.

I am on an embankment somewhere.

Why am I on the embankment?

But it wasn't the way a man thought, at least not the normal way a normal man would think. Man thought in shortcuts. He cut across the block and did not go all the way around.

It was a frightening thing, he told himself, this clear-around-the-block thinking. It wasn't normal and it wasn't right and it made no sense at all. . . no more sense than did the fact that he should find himself in a place with no memory of getting there.

He rose to his feet and ran his hands up and down his body. His clothes were neat, not rumpled. He hadn't been beaten up and he hadn't been thrown from a speeding car. There were no sore places on his body and his face was unbloody and whole and he felt all right.

He hooked his fingers in the holster belt and shucked it up so that it rode tightly on his hips. He pulled out the gun and checked it with expert and familiar fingers and the gun was ready.

He walked up the embankment and reached the road, went across it with a swinging stride to reach the sidewalk that fronted the row of new bungalows. He heard a car coming and stepped off the sidewalk to crouch in a clump of evergreen that landscaped one corner of a lawn. The move was instinctive and he crouched there, feeling just a little foolish at the thing he'd done.

The car went past and no one saw him. They would not, he now realized, have noticed him even if he had remained out on the sidewalk.

He was unsure of himself; that must be the reason for his fear. There was a blank spot in his life, some mysterious incident that he did not know and the unknowing of it had undermined the sure and solid foundation of his own existence, had wrecked the basis of his motive and had turned him, momentarily, into a furtive animal that darted and hid at the approach of his fellow men.

That and something that had happened to him that made him think clear around the block.

He remained crouching in the evergreens, watching the street and the stretch of sidewalk, conscious of the white-painted, ghostly bungalows squatting back in their landscaped lots.

A word came into his mind. *Puudly.* An odd word, unearthly, yet it held terror.

The *puudly* had escaped and that was why he was here, hiding on the front lawn of some unsuspecting and sleeping citizen, equipped with a gun and a determination to use it, ready to match his wits and the quickness of brain and muscle against the most bloodthirsty, hate-filled thing yet found in the Galaxy.

The *puudly* was dangerous. It was not a thing to harbor. In fact, there was a law against harboring not only a *puudly*, but certain other alien beasties even less lethal than a *puudly*. There was good reason for such a law, reason which no one, much less himself, would ever think to question.

And now the *puudly* was loose and somewhere in the city.

James grew cold at the thought of it, his brain forming images of the things that might come to pass if he did not hunt down the alien beast and put an end to it.

Although beast was not quite the word to use. The *puudly* was more than a beast. . . just how much more than a beast he once had hoped to learn. He had not learned a lot, he now admitted to himself, not nearly all there was to learn, but he had learned enough. More than enough to frighten him.

For one thing, he had learned what hate could be and how shallow an emotion human hate turned out when measured against the depth and intensity and the ravening horror of the *puudly's* hate. Not unreasoning hate, for unreasoning hate defeats itself, but a rational, calculating, driving hate that motivated a clever and deadly killing machine which directed its rapacity and its cunning against every living thing that was not a *puudly*.

For the beast had a mind and a personality that operated upon the basic law of self-preservation against all comers, whoever they might be, extending that law to the interpretation that safety lay in one direction only. . . the death of every other living being. No other reason was needed for a *puudly*'s killing. The fact that anything else lived and moved and was thus posing a threat, no matter how remote, against a *puudly*, was sufficient reason in itself.

It was psychotic, of course, some murderous instinct planted far back in time and deep in the creature's racial consciousness, but no more psychotic, perhaps, than many human instincts.

The *puudly* had been, and still was for that matter, a unique opportunity for a study in alien behaviorism. Given a permit, one could have studied them on their native planet. Refused a permit, one sometimes did a foolish thing, as James had.

And foolish acts backfire, as this one did.

James put down a hand and patted the gun at his side, as if by doing so he might derive some assurance that he was equal to the task. There was no question in his mind as to the thing that must be done. He must find the *puudly* and kill it and he must do that before the break of dawn. Anything less than that would be abject and horrifying failure.

For the *puudly* would bud. It was long past its time for the reproductive act and there were bare hours left to find it before it had loosed upon the Earth dozens of baby *puudlies*. They would not remain babies for long. A few hours after budding they would strike out on their own.

To find one *puudly*, lost in the vastness of a sleeping city, seemed bad enough; to track down some dozens of them would be impossible.

So it was tonight or never.

Tonight there would be no killing on the *puudly*'s part. Tonight the beast would be intent on one thing only, to find a place where it could rest in quiet, where it could give itself over, wholeheartedly and with no interference, to the business of bringing other *puudlies* into being.

It was clever. It would have known where it was going before it had escaped. There would be, on its part, no time wasted in seeking or in doubling back. It would have known where it was going and already it was there, already the buds would be rising on its body, bursting forth and growing.

There was one place, and one place only, in the entire city where an alien beast would be safe from prying eyes. A man could figure that one out and so could a *puudly*. The question was: Would the *puudly* know that man could figure it out? Would the *puudly* underestimate a man? Or, knowing that the man would know it, too, would it find another place of hiding?

James rose from the evergreens and went down the sidewalk. The street marker at the corner, standing underneath a swinging street light, told him where he was and it was closer to the place where he was going than he might have hoped.

The zoo was quiet for a while, and then something sent up a howl that raised James' hackles and made his blood stop in his veins.

James, having scaled the fence, stood tensely at its foot, trying to identify the howling animal. He was unable to place it. More than likely, he told himself, it was a new one. A person simply couldn't keep track of all the zoo's occupants. New ones were coming in all the time, strange, unheard-of creatures from the distant stars.

Straight ahead lay the unoccupied moat cage that up until a day or two before had held an unbelievable monstrosity from the jungles of one of the Arctian worlds. James grimaced in the dark, remembering the thing. They had finally had to kill it.

And now the *puudly* was there. . . well, maybe not there, but one place that it could be, the one place in the entire city where it might be seen and arouse no comment, for the zoo was filled with animals that were seldom seen and another strange one would arouse only momentary wonder. One animal more would go unnoticed unless some zoo attendant should think to check the records.

There, in that unoccupied cage area, the *puudly* would be undisturbed, could quietly go about its business of budding out more *puudlies*. No one would bother it, for things like *puudlies* were the normal occupants of this place set aside for the strangers brought to Earth to be stared at and studied by that ferocious race, the humans.

James stood quietly beside the fence.

Henderson James. Thirty-six. Unmarried. Alien psychologist. An official of this zoo. And an offender against the law for having secured and harbored an alien being that was barred from Earth.

Why, he asked himself, did he think of himself in this way? Why, standing here, did he catalogue himself? It was instinctive to know one's self. . . there was no need, no sense of setting up a mental outline of one's self.

It had been foolish to go ahead with the *puudly* business. He recalled how he had spent days fighting it out with himself, reviewing all the disastrous possibilities which might arise from it. If the old renegade spaceman had not come to him and had not said, over a bottle of most delicious Lupan wine, that he could deliver, for a certain, rather staggering sum, one live *puudly*, in good condition, it never would have happened.

James was sure that of himself he never would have

thought of it. But the old space captain was a man he knew and admired from former dealings. He was a man who was not averse to turning either an honest or a dishonest dollar, and yet he was a man, for all of that, you could depend upon. He would do what you paid him for and keep his lip buttoned tight once the deed was done.

James had wanted a *puudly*, for it was a most engaging beast with certain little tricks that, once understood, might open up new avenues of speculation and approach, might write new chapters in the tortuous study of alien minds and manners.

But for all of that, it had been a terrifying thing to do and now that the beast was loose, the terror was compounded. For it was not wholly beyond speculation that the descendants of this one brood that the escaped *puudly* would spawn might wipe out the population of the Earth, or at the best, make the Earth untenable for its rightful dwellers.

A place like the Earth, with its teeming millions, would provide a field day for the fangs of the *puudlies*, and the minds that drove the fangs. They would not hunt for hunger, nor for the sheer madness of the kill, but because of the compelling conviction that no *puudly* would be safe until Earth was wiped clean of life. They would be killing for survival, as a cornered rat would kill. . . except that they would be cornered nowhere but in the murderous insecurity of their minds.

If the posses scoured the Earth to hunt them down, they would be found in all directions, for they would be shrewd enough to scatter. They would know the ways of guns and traps and poisons and there would be more and more of them as time went on. Each of them would accelerate its budding to replace with a dozen or a hundred the ones that might be killed.

James moved quietly forward to the edge of the moat and let himself down into the mud that covered the bottom. When the monstrosity had been killed, the moat had been drained and should long since have been cleaned, but the press of work, James thought, must have prevented its getting done.

Slowly he waded out into the mud, feeling his way, his feet making sucking noises as he pulled them through the slime. Finally he reached the rocky incline that led out of the moat to the island cage.

He stood for a moment, his hands on the great, wet boulders, listening, trying to hold his breath so the sound of it would not interfere with hearing. The thing that howled had quieted and the night was deathly quiet. Or seemed, at first, to be. Then he heard the little insect noises that ran through the grass and bushes and the whisper of the leaves in the trees across the moat and the far-off sound that was the hoarse breathing of a sleeping city.

Now, for the first time, he felt fear. Felt it in the silence that was not a silence, in the mud beneath his feet, in the upthrust boulders that rose out of the moat.

The *puudly* was a dangerous thing, not only because it was strong and quick, but because it was intelligent. Just how intelligent, he did not know. It reasoned and it planned and schemed. It could talk, though not as a human talks. . . probably better than a human ever could. For it not only could talk words, but it could talk emotions. It lured its victims to it by the thoughts it put into their minds; it held them entranced with dreams and illusion until it slit their throats. It could purr a man to sleep, could lull him to suicidal inaction. It could drive him crazy with a single flickering thought, hurling a perception so foul and alien that the mind recoiled deep inside itself and stayed there, coiled tight, like a watch that has been overwound and will not run.

It should have budded long ago, but it had fought off its budding, holding back against the day when it might escape, planning, he realized now, its fight to stay on Earth, which meant its conquest of Earth. It had planned, and planned well, against this very moment, and it would feel or show no mercy to anyone who interfered with it.

His hand went down and touched the gun and he felt the muscles in his jaw involuntarily tightening and suddenly there was at once a lightness and a hardness in him that had not been there before. He pulled himself up the boulder face, seeking cautious hand- and toeholds, breathing shallowly, body pressed against the rock. Quickly, and surely, and no noise, for he must reach the top and be there before the *puudly* knew there was anyone around.

The *puudly* would be relaxed and intent upon its business, engrossed in the budding forth of that numerous family that in days to come would begin the grim and relentless crusade to make an alien planet safe for *puudlies*. . . and for *puudlies* alone.

That is, if the *puudly* were here and not somewhere else. James was only a human trying to think like a *puudly* and that was not an easy or a pleasant job and he had no way of knowing if he succeeded. He could only hope that his reasoning was vicious and crafty enough.

His clawing hand found grass and earth and he sank his fingers deep into the soil, hauling his body up the last few feet of the rock face above the pit.

He lay flat upon the gently sloping ground, listening, tensed for any danger. He studied the ground in front of him, probing every foot. Distant street lamps lighting the zoo walks threw back the total blackness that had engulfed him as he climbed out of the moat, but there still were areas of shadow that he had to study closely.

Inch by inch, he squirmed his way along, making sure of the terrain immediately ahead before he moved a muscle. He held the gun in a rock-hard fist, ready for instant action, watching for the faintest hint of motion, alert for any hump or irregularity that was not rock or bush or grass.

Minutes magnified themselves into hours, his eyes

ached with staring and the lightness that had been in him drained away, leaving only the hardness, which was as tense as a drawn bowstring. A sense of failure began to seep into his mind and with it came the full-fledged, until now unadmitted, realization of what failure meant, not only for the world, but for the dignity and the pride that was Henderson James.

Now, faced with the possibility, he admitted to himself the action he must take if the *puudly* were not here, if he did not find it here and kill it. He would have to notify the authorities, would have to attempt to alert the police, must plead with newspapers and radio to warn the citizenry, must reveal himself as a man who, through pride and self-conceit, had exposed the people of the Earth to this threat against their hold upon their native planet.

They would not believe him. They would laugh at him until the laughter died in their torn throats, choked off with their blood. He sweated, thinking of it, thinking of the price this city, and the world, would pay before it learned the truth.

There was a whisper of sound, a movement of black against deeper black.

The *puudly* rose in front of him, not more than six feet away, from its bed beside a bush. He jerked the pistol up and his finger tightened on the trigger.

"Don't," the *puudly* said inside his mind. "I'll go along with you."

His finger strained with the careful slowness of the squeeze and the gun leaped in his hand, but even as it did he felt the whiplash of terror slash at his brain, caught for just a second the terrible import, the mind-shattering obscenity that glanced off his mind and ricocheted away.

"Too late," he told the *puudly*, with his voice and his mind and his body shaking. "You should have tried that first. You wasted precious seconds. You would have got me if you had done it first."

It had been easy, he assured himself, much easier than he had thought. The *puudly* was dead or dying and the Earth and its millions of unsuspecting citizens were safe, and, best of all, Henderson James was safe. . . safe from indignity, safe from being stripped naked of the little defenses he had built up through the years to shield him against the public stare. He felt relief flood over him and it left him pulseless and breathless and feeling clean, but weak.

"You fool," the dying *puudly* said, death clouding its words as they built up in his mind. "You fool, you half-thing, you duplicate. . ."

It died then and he felt it die, felt the life go out of it and leave it empty.

He rose softly to his feet and he seemed stunned and at first he thought it was from knowing death, from having touched hands with death within the *puudly*'s mind.

The *puudly* had tried to fool him. Faced with the pistol, it had tried to throw him off his balance to give it the second that it needed to hurl the mind-blasting thought that had caught at the edge of his brain. If he had hesitated for a moment, he knew, it would have been all over with him. If his finger had slacked for a moment, it would have been too late.

The *puudly* must have known that he would think of the zoo as the first logical place to look and, even knowing that, it had held him in enough contempt to come here, had not even bothered to try to watch for him, had not tried to stalk him, had waited until he was almost on top of it before it moved.

And that was queer, for the *puudly* must have known, with its uncanny mental powers, every move that he had made. It must have maintained a casual contact with his mind every second of the time since it had escaped. He had known that and. . . wait a minute, he hadn't known it until this very moment, although, knowing it now, it seemed as if he had always known it.

What is the matter with me, he thought. There's something wrong with me. I should have known I could not surprise the *puudly*, and yet I didn't know it. I must have surprised it, for otherwise it would have finished me off quite leisurely at any moment after I climbed out of the moat.

You fool, the *puudly* had said. You fool, you half-thing, you duplicate. . .

You duplicate!

He felt the strength and the personality and the hard, unquestioned identity of himself as Henderson James, human being, drain out of him, as if someone had cut the puppet string and he, the puppet, had slumped supine upon the stage.

So that was why he had been able to surprise the *puudly!*

There were two Henderson Jameses. The *puudly* had been in contact with one of them, the original, the real Henderson James, had known every move he made, had known that it was safe so far as that Henderson James might be concerned. It had not known of the second Henderson James that had stalked it through the night.

Henderson James, duplicate.

Henderson James, temporary.

Henderson James, here tonight, gone tomorrow.

For they would not let him live. The original Henderson James would not allow him to continue living, and even if he did, the world would not allow it. Duplicates were made only for very temporary and very special reasons and it was always understood that once their purpose was accomplished they would be done away with.

Done away with. . . those were the words exactly. Gotten out of the way. Swept out of sight and mind. Killed as unconcernedly and emotionlessly as one chops off a chicken's head.

He walked forward and dropped on one knee beside the *puudly*, running his hand over its body in the darkness. Lumps stood out all over it, the swelling buds that now would never break to spew forth in a loathsome birth a brood of *puudly* pups.

He rose to his feet.

The job was done. The *puudly* had been killed—killed before it had given birth to a horde of horrors.

The job was done and he could go home.

Home?

Of course, that was the thing that had been planted in his mind, the thing they wanted him to do. To go home, to go back to the house on Summit Avenue, where his executioners would wait, to walk back deliberately and unsuspectingly to the death that waited.

The job was done and his usefulness was over. He had been created to perform a certain task and the task was now performed and while an hour ago he had been a factor in the plans of men, he was no longer wanted. He was an embarrassment and superfluous.

Now wait a minute, he told himself. You may not be a duplicate. You do not feel like one.

That was true. He felt like Henderson James. He was Henderson James. He lived on Summit Avenue and had illegally brought to Earth a beast known as a *puudly* in order that he might study it and talk to it and test its alien reactions, attempt to measure its intelligence and guess at the strength and depth and the direction of its non-humanity. He had been a fool, of course, to do it, and yet at the time it had seemed important to understand the deadly, alien mentality.

I am human, he said, and that was right, but even so the fact meant nothing. Of course he was human. Henderson James was human and his duplicate would be exactly as human as the original. For the duplicate, processed from the pattern that held every trait and characteristic of the man he was to become a copy of, would differ in not a single basic factor.

In not a single basic factor, perhaps, but in certain other things. For no matter how much the duplicate might be like his pattern, no matter how full-limbed he might spring from his creation, he still would be a new man. He would have the capacity for knowledge and for thought and in a little time he would have and know and be all the things that his original was. . .

But it would take some time, some short while to come to a full realization of all he knew and was, some time to coordinate and recognize all the knowledge and experience that lay within his mind. At first he'd grope and search until he came upon the things that he must know. Until he became acquainted with himself, with the sort of man he was, he could not reach out blindly in the dark and put his hand exactly and unerringly upon the thing he wished.

That had been exactly what he'd done. He had groped and searched. He had been compelled to think, at first, in simple basic truths and facts.

I am a man.

I am on a planet called Earth.

I am Henderson James.

I live on Summit Avenue.

There is a job to do.

It had been quite a while, he remembered now, before he had been able to dig out of his mind the nature of the job.

There is a *puudly* to hunt down and destroy.

Even now he could not find in the hidden, still-veiled recesses of his mind the many valid reasons why a man should run so grave a risk to study a thing so vicious as a *puudly*. There were reasons, he knew there were, and in a little time he would know them quite specifically.

The point was that if he were Henderson James, original, he would know them now, know them as a part of himself and his life, without laboriously searching for them.

The *puudly* had known, of course. It had known, beyond any chance of error, that there were two Henderson Jameses. It had been keeping tab on one when another one showed up. A mentality far less astute than the *puudly*'s would have had no trouble in figuring that one out.

If the *puudly* had not talked, he told himself, I never would have known. If it had died at once and not had a chance to taunt me, I would not have known. I would even now be walking to the house on Summit Avenue.

He stood lonely and naked of soul in the wind that swept across the moated island. There was a sour bitterness in his mouth.

He moved a foot and touched the dead *puudly*.

"I'm sorry," he told the stiffening body. "I'm sorry now I did it. If I had known, I never would have killed you."

Stiffly erect, he moved away.

He stopped at the street corner, keeping well in the shadow. Halfway down the block, and on the other side, was the house. A light burned in one of the rooms upstairs and another on the post beside the gate that opened into the yard, lighting the walk up to the door.

Just as if, he told himself, the house were waiting for the master to come home. And that, of course, was exactly what it was doing. An old lady of a house, waiting, hands folded in its lap, rocking very gently in a squeaky chair. . . and with a gun beneath the folded shawl.

His lip lifted in half a snarl as he stood there, looking at the house. What do they take me for, he thought, putting out a trap in plain sight and one that's not even baited? Then he remembered. They would not know, of course, that he knew he was a duplicate. They would think that he would think that he was Henderson James, the one and only. They would expect him to come walking home, quite naturally, believing he belonged there. So far as they would know, there would be no possibility of his finding out the truth.

And now that he had? Now that he was here, across the street from the waiting house?

He had been brought into being, had been given life, to do a job that his original had not dared to do, or had not wanted to do. He had carried out a killing his original didn't want to dirty his hands with, or risk his neck in doing.

Or had it not been that at all, but the necessity of two men working on the job, the original serving as a focus for the *puudly*'s watchful mind while the other man sneaked up to kill it while it watched?

No matter what, he had been created, at a good stiff price, from the pattern of the man that was Henderson James. The wizardry of man's knowledge, the magic of machines, a deep understanding of organic chemistry, of human physiology, of the mystery of life, had made a second Henderson James. It was legal, of course, under certain circumstances. . . for example, in the case of public policy, and his own creation, he knew, might have been validated under such a heading. But there were conditions and one of these was that a duplicate not be allowed to continue living once it had served the specific purpose for which it had been created.

Usually such a condition was a simple one to carry out, for the duplicate was not meant to know he was a duplicate. So far as he was concerned, he was the original. There was no suspicion in him, no foreknowledge of the doom that was invariably ordered for him, no reason for him to be on guard against the death that waited.

The duplicate knitted his brow, trying to puzzle it out.

There was a strange set of ethics here.

He was alive and he wanted to stay alive. Life, once it had been tasted, was too sweet, too good, to go back to the nothingness from which he had come. . . or would it be nothingness? Now that he had known life, now that he was alive, might he not hope for a life after death, the same as any other human being? Might not he, too, have the same human right as any other human to grasp at the shadowy and glorious promises and assurances held out by religion and by faith?

He tried to marshal what he knew about those promises and assurances, but his knowledge was illusive. A little later he would remember more about it. A little later, when the neural bookkeeper in his mind had been able to coordinate and activate the knowledge that he had inherited from the pattern, he would know.

He felt a trace of anger stir deep inside of him, anger at the unfairness of allowing him only a few short hours of life, of allowing him to learn how wonderful a thing life was, only to snatch it from him. It was a cruelty that went beyond mere human cruelty. It was something that had been fashioned out of the distorted perspective of a machine society that measured existence only in terms of mechanical and physical worth, that discarded with a ruthless hand whatever part of that society had no specific purpose.

The cruelty, he told himself, was in ever giving life, not in taking it away.

His original, of course, was the one to blame. He was the one who had obtained the *puudly* and allowed it to escape. It was his fumbling and his inability to correct his error without help which had created the necessity of fashioning a duplicate.

And yet, could he blame him?

Perhaps, rather, he owed him gratitude for a few hours of life at least, gratitude for the privilege of knowing what life was like. Although he could not quite decide whether or not it was something which called for gratitude.

He stood there, staring at the house. That light in the upstairs room was in the study off the master bedroom.

Up there Henderson James, original, was waiting for the word that the duplicate had come home to death. It was an easy thing to sit there and wait, to sit and wait for the word that was sure to come. An easy thing to sentence to death a man one had never seen, even if that man be the walking image of one's self.

It would be a harder decision to kill him if you stood face to face with him. . . harder to kill someone who would be, of necessity, closer than a brother, someone who would be, even literally, flesh of your flesh, blood of your blood, brain of your brain.

There would be a practical side as well, a great advantage to be able to work with a man who thought as you did, who would be almost a second self. It would be almost as if there were two of you.

A thing like that could be arranged. Plastic surgery and a price for secrecy could make your duplicate into an unrecognizable other person. A little red tape, some finagling. . . but it could be done. It was a proposition that Henderson James, duplicate, thought would interest Henderson James, original. Or at least he hoped it would.

The room with the light could be reached with a little luck, with strength and agility and determination. The brick expanse of a chimney, its base cloaked by shrubs, its length masked by a closely growing tree, ran up the wall. A man could climb its rough brick face, could reach out and swing himself through the open window into the lighted room.

And once Henderson James, original, stood face to face with Henderson James, duplicate. . . well, it would be less of a gamble. The duplicate then would no longer be an impersonal factor. He would be a man and one that was very close to his original.

There would be watchers, but they would be watching the front door. If he were quiet, if he could reach and climb the chimney without making any noise, he'd be in the room before anyone would notice.

He drew back deeper in the shadows and considered. It was either get into the room and face his original, hope to be able to strike a compromise with him, or simply to light out. . . to run and hide and wait, watching his chance to get completely away, perhaps to some far planet in some other part of the Galaxy.

Both ways were a gamble, but one was quick, would either succeed or fail within the hour; the other might drag on for months with a man never knowing whether he was safe, never being sure.

Something nagged at him, a persistent little fact that skittered through his brain and eluded his efforts to pin it down. It might be important and then, again, it might be a random thing, simply a floating piece of information that was looking for its pigeonhole.

His mind shrugged it off.

The quick way or the long way?

He stood thinking for a moment and then moved swiftly down the street, seeking a place where he could cross in shadow.

He had chosen the short way.

The room was empty.

He stood beside the window, quietly, only his eyes moving, searching every corner, checking against a situation that couldn't seem quite true. . . that Henderson James was not here, waiting for the word.

Then he strode swiftly to the bedroom door and swung it open. His finger found the switch and the lights went on. The bedroom was empty and so was the bath. He went back into the study.

He stood with his back against the wall, facing the door that led into the hallway, but his eyes went over the room, foot by foot, orienting himself, feeling himself flow into the shape and form of it, feeling familiarity creep in upon him and enfold him in its comfort of belonging.

Here were the books, the fireplace with its mantel

loaded with souvenirs, the easy chairs, the liquor cabinet. . . and all were a part of him, a background that was as much a part of Henderson James as his body and his inner thoughts were a part of him.

This, he thought, is what I would have missed, the experience I never would have had if the *puudly* had not taunted me. I would have died an empty and unrelated body that had no actual place in the universe.

The phone purred at him and he stood there startled by it, as if some intruder from the outside had pushed its way into the room, shattering the sense of belonging that had come to him.

The phone rang again and he went across the room and picked it up.

"James speaking," he said.

"That you, Mr. James?"

The voice was that of Anderson, the gardener.

"Why, yes," said the duplicate. "Who did you think it was?"

"We got a fellow here who says he's you."

Henderson James, duplicate, stiffened with fright and his hand, suddenly, was grasping the phone so hard that he found the time to wonder why it did not pulverize to bits beneath his fingers.

"He's dressed like you," the gardener said, "and I knew you went out. Talked to you, remember? Told you that you shouldn't? Not with us waiting for that. . . that thing."

"Yes," said the duplicate, his voice so even that he could not believe it was he who spoke. "Yes, certainly I remember talking with you."

"But, sir, how did you get back?"

"I came in the back way," the even voice said into the phone. "Now what's holding you back?"

"He's dressed like you."

"Naturally. Of course he would be, Anderson."

And that, to be sure, didn't quite follow, but Anderson wasn't too bright to start with and now he was somewhat upset.

"You remember," the duplicate said, "that we talked about it."

"I guess I was excited and forgot," admitted Anderson. "You told me to call you, to make sure you were in your study, though. That's right, isn't it?"

"You've called me," the duplicate said, "and I am here."

"Then the other one out here is him?"

"Of course," said the duplicate. "Who else could it be?"

He put the phone back into the cradle and stood waiting. It came a moment after, the dull throaty cough of a gun.

He walked to a chair and sank into it, spent with the knowledge of how events had so been ordered that now, finally, he was safe, safe beyond all question.

Soon he would have to change into other clothes, hide the gun and the clothes that he was wearing. The staff would ask no questions, most likely, but it was best to let nothing arouse suspicion in their minds.

He felt his nerves quieting and he allowed himself to glance about the room, take in the books and furnishings, the soft and easy. . . and earned. . . comfort of a man solidly and unshakably established in the world.

He smiled softly.

"It will be nice," he said.

It had been easy. Now that it was over, it seemed ridiculously easy. Easy because he had never seen the man who had walked up to the door. It was easy to kill a man you have never seen.

With each passing hour he would slip deeper and deeper into the personality that was his by right of heritage. There would be no one to question, after a time not even himself, that he was Henderson James.

The phone rang again and he got up to answer it.

A pleasant voice told him, "This is Allen, over at the duplication lab. We've been waiting for a report from you."

"Well," said James, "I. . ."

"I just called," interrupted Allen, "to tell you not to worry. It slipped my mind before."

"I see," said James, though he didn't.

"We did this one a little differently," Allen explained. "An experiment that we thought we'd try out. Slow poison in his bloodstream. Just another precaution. Probably not necessary, but we like to be positive. In case he fails to show up, you needn't worry any."

"I am sure he will show up."

Allen chuckled. "Twenty-four hours. Like a time bomb. No antidote for it even if he found out somehow."

"It was good of you to let me know," said James.

"Glad to," said Allen. "Good night, Mr. James."

Dusty Zebra

If you're human, you can't keep a thing around the house. You're always losing things and never finding them and you go charging through the place, yelling, cross-examining, blaming.

That's the way it is in all families.

Just one warning—don't try to figure out where all those things have gone or who might have taken them. If you have any notion of investigating, forget it. You'll be happier!

I'll tell you how it was with me.

I'd bought the sheet of stamps on my way home from the office so I could mail out the checks for the monthly bills. But I'd just sat down to write the checks when Marge and Lewis Shaw dropped over. I don't care much for Lewis and he barely tolerates me. But Marge and Helen are good friends, and they got to talking, and the Shaws stayed all evening.

Lewis told me about the work he was doing at his research laboratory out at the edge of town. I tried to switch him off to something else, but he kept right on. I suppose he's so interested in his work that he figures everyone else must be. But I don't know a thing about electronics and I can't tell a microgauge from a microscope.

It was a fairly dismal evening and the worst of it was that I couldn't say so. Helen would have jumped all over me for being antisocial.

So, the next evening after dinner, I went into the den to write the checks and, of course, the stamps were gone.

I had left the sheet on top of the desk and now the desk was bare except for one of the Bildo-Blocks that young Bill had outgrown several years before, but which still turn up every now and then in the most unlikely places.

I looked around the room. Just in case they might have blown off the desk, I got down on my hands and knees and searched under everything. There was no sign of the stamps.

I went into the living room, where Helen was curled up in a chair, watching television.

"I haven't seen them, Joe," she said. "They must be where you left them."

It was exactly the kind of answer I should have expected.

"Bill might know," I said.

"He's scarcely been in the house all day. When he does show up, you've got to speak to him."

"What's the matter now?"

"It's this trading business. He traded off that new belt we got him for a pair of spurs."

"I can't see anything wrong in that. When I was a kid. . ."

"It's not just the belt," she said. "He's traded everything. And the worst of it is that he always seems to get the best of it."

"The kid's smart."

"If you take that attitude, Joe. . ."

"It's not *my* attitude," I said. "It's the attitude of the whole business world. When Bill grows up. . ."

"When he grows up, he'll be in prison. Why, the way

he trades, you'd swear he was training to be a con man!"

"All right, I'll talk to him."

I went back into the den because the atmosphere wasn't exactly as friendly as it might have been and, anyhow, I had to send out those checks, stamps or no stamps.

I got the pile of bills and the checkbook and the fountain pen out of the drawer. I reached out and picked up the Bildo-Block to put it to one side, so I'd have a good, clear space to work on. But the moment I picked it up, I knew that this thing was no Bildo-Block.

It was the right size and weight and was black and felt like plastic, except that it was slicker than any plastic I had ever felt. It felt as if it had oil on it, only it didn't.

I set it down in front of me and pulled the desk lamp closer. But there wasn't much to see. It still looked like one of the Bildo-Blocks.

Turning it around, I tried to make out what it was. On the second turn, I saw the faint oblong depression along one side of it—a very shallow depression, almost like a scratch.

I looked at it a little closer and could see that the depression was machined and that within it was a faint red line. I could have sworn the red line flickered just a little. I held it there, studying it, and could detect no further flicker. Either the red had faded or I had been seeing things to start with, for after a few seconds I couldn't be sure there was any line at all.

I figured it must have been something Bill had picked up or traded for. The kid is more than half pack-rat, but there's nothing wrong with that, nor with the trading, either, for all that Helen says. It's just the first signs of good business sense.

I put the block over to one side of the desk and went on with the checks. The next day, during lunch hour, I bought some more stamps so I could mail them. And off and on, all day, I wondered what could have happened to that sheet of stamps.

I didn't think at all about the block that had the oily feel. Possibly I would have forgotten it entirely, except that when I got home, the fountain pen was missing.

I went into the den to get the pen and there the pen was, lying on top of the desk where I'd left it the night before. Not that I remembered leaving it there. But when I saw it there, I remembered having forgotten to put it back into the drawer.

I picked it up. It wasn't any pen. It felt like a cylinder of cork, but much too heavy to be any kind of cork. Except that it was heavier and smaller, it felt something—somehow—like a fly rod.

Thinking of how a fly rod felt, I gave my hand a twitch, the way you do to cast a line, and suddenly it seemed to be, in fact, a fly rod. It apparently had been telescoped and now it came untelescoped and lengthened out into what might have been a rod. But the funny thing about it was that it went out only about four feet and then disappeared into thin air.

Instinctively, I brought it up and back to free the tip from wherever it might be. I felt the slack take up against a sudden weight and I knew I had something on the other end of it. Just like a fish feels, only it wasn't fighting.

Then, as quickly as it happened, it unhappened. I felt the tension snap off and the weight at the other end was gone and the rod had telescoped again and I held in my hand the thing that looked like a fountain pen.

I laid it down carefully on the desk, being very certain to make no more casting motions, and it wasn't until then that I saw my hand was shaking.

I sat down, goggling at the thing that looked like the missing fountain pen and the other thing that looked like a Bildo-Block.

And it was then, while I was looking at the two of them, that I saw, out of the corner of my eye, the little white dot in the center of the desk.

It was on the exact spot where the bogus pen had lain and more than likely, I imagined, the exact spot where I'd found the Bildo-Block the night before. It was about a quarter of an inch in diameter and it looked like ivory.

I put out my thumb and rubbed it vigorously, but the dot would not rub off. I closed my eyes so the dot would have a chance to go away, and then opened them again, real quick, to surprise it if it hadn't. It still was there.

I bent over the desk to examine it. I could see it was inlaid in the wood, and an excellent job of inlaying, too. I couldn't find even the faintest line of division between the wood and the dot.

It hadn't been there before; I was sure of that. If it had been, I would have noticed it. What's more, Helen would have noticed it, for she's hell on dirt and forever after things with a dusting cloth. And to cinch the fact that it had not been there before, no one I ever heard of sold desks with single inlaid ivory dots.

And no one sold a thing that looked like a fountain pen but could become a fly rod, the business end of which disappeared and hooked a thing you couldn't even see—and which, the next time, might bring in whatever it had caught instead of losing it.

Helen called to me from the living room. "Joe."

"Yeah. What is it?"

"Did you talk to Bill?"

"Bill? About what?"

"About the trading."

"No. I guess I forgot."

"Well, you'll have to. He's at it again. He traded Jimmy out of that new bicycle. Gave him a lot of junk. I made him give back the bicycle."

"I'll have a talk with him," I promised again.

But I'm afraid I wasn't paying as close attention to the ethics of the situation as I should have been.

You couldn't keep a thing around the house. You were

always losing this or that. You knew just where you'd put it and you were sure it was there and then, when you went to look for it, it had disappeared.

It was happening everywhere—things being lost and never turning up.

But other things weren't left in their places—at least not that you heard about.

Although maybe there had been times when things had been left that a man might pick up and examine and not know what they were and puzzle over, then toss in a corner somewhere and forget.

Maybe, I thought, the junkyards of the world were loaded with outlandish blocks and crazy fishing rods.

I got up and went into the living room, where Helen had turned on the television set.

She must have seen that something had me upset, because she asked, "What's the matter now?"

"I can't find the fountain pen."

She laughed at me. "Honestly, Joe, you're the limit. You're always losing things."

That night, I lay awake after Helen went to sleep and all I could think about was the dot upon the desk. A dot, perhaps, that said, *Put it right here, pardner, and we will make a swap.*

And, thinking of it, I wondered what would happen if someone moved the desk.

I lay there for a long time, trying not to worry, trying to tell myself it didn't matter, that I was insane to think what I was thinking.

But I couldn't get it out of my mind.

So I finally got up and sneaked out of the bedroom and, feeling like a thief in my own house, headed for the den.

I closed the door, turned on the desk lamp and took a quick look to see if the dot was still there.

It was.

I opened the desk drawer and hunted for a pencil and

couldn't find one, but I finally found one of Bill's crayons. I got down on my knees and carefully marked the floor around the desk legs, so that, if the desk were moved, I could put it back again.

Then, pretending I had no particular purpose for doing it, I laid the crayon precisely on the dot.

In the morning, I sneaked a look into the den and the crayon was still there. I went to work a little easier in my mind, for by then I'd managed to convince myself that it was all imagination.

But that evening, after dinner, I went back into the den and the crayon was gone.

In its place was a triangular contraption with what appeared to be lenses set in each angle, and with a framework of some sort of metal, holding in place what apparently was a suction cup in the center of the triangle.

While I was looking at it, Helen came to the door.

"Marge and I are going to see a movie," she said. "Why don't you go over and have a beer with Lewis?"

"With that stuffed shirt?"

"What's the matter with Lewis?"

"Nothing, I guess." I didn't feel up to a family row right then.

"What's that you've got?" she asked.

"I don't know. Just something I found."

"Well, don't *you* start bringing home all sorts of junk, the way Bill does. One of you is enough to clutter up the house."

I sat there, looking at the triangle, and the only thing I could figure out was that it might be a pair of glasses. The suction cup in the center might hold it on the wearer's face and, while that might seem a funny way to wear a pair of glasses, it made sense when you thought about it. But if that were true, it meant that the wearer had three eyes, set in a triangle in his face.

I sat around for quite a while after Helen left, doing a

lot of thinking. And what I was thinking was that even if I didn't care too much about Lewis, he was the only man I knew who might be able to help me out.

So I put the bogus fountain pen and the three-eyed glasses in the drawer and put the counterfeit Bildo-Block in my pocket and went across the street.

Lewis had a bunch of blueprints spread out on the kitchen table, and he started to explain them to me. I did the best I could to act as if I understood them. Actually, I didn't know head nor tail of it.

Finally, I was able to get a word in edgewise and I pulled the block out of my pocket and put it on the table.

"What is that?" I asked.

I expected him to say right off it was just a child's block. But he didn't. There must have been something about it to tip him off that it wasn't just a simple block. That comes, of course, of having a technical education.

Lewis picked the block up and turned it around in his fingers. "What's it made of?" he asked me, sounding excited.

I shook my head. "I don't know what it is or what it's made of or anything about it. I just found it."

"This is something I've never seen before." Then he spotted the depression in one side of it and I could see I had him hooked. "Let me take it down to the shop. We'll see what we can learn."

I knew what he was after, of course. If the block was something new, he wanted a chance to go over it—but that didn't bother me any. I had a hunch he wouldn't find out too much about it.

We had a couple more beers and I went home. I hunted up an old pair of spectacles and put them on the desk right over the dot.

I was listening to the news when Helen came in. She said she was glad I'd spent the evening with Lewis, that I should try to get to know him better and that, once I got to know him better, I might like him. She said, since she and Marge were such good friends, it was a shame Lewis and I didn't hit it off.

"Maybe we will," I said and let it go at that.

The next afternoon, Lewis called me at the office.

"Where'd you get that thing?" he asked.

"Found it," I said.

"Have any idea what it is?"

"Nope," I told him cheerfully. "That's why I gave it to you."

"It's powered in some way and it's meant to measure something. That depression in the side must be a gauge. Color seems to be used as an indicator. At any rate, the color line in the depression keeps changing all the time. Not much, but enough so you can say there's some change."

"Next thing is to find out what it's measuring."

"Joe, do you know where you can get another of them?"

"No, I don't."

"It's this way," he said. "We'd like to get into this one, to see what makes it tick, but we can't find any way to open it. We could break into it, probably, but we're afraid to do that. We might damage it. Or it might explode. If we had another. . ."

He had to let it go at that.

I went home that evening grinning to myself, thinking about Lewis. The guy was fit to be tied. He wouldn't sleep until he found out what the thing was, now that he'd started on it. It probably would keep him out of my hair for a week or so.

I went into the den. The glasses still were on the desk. I stood there for a moment, looking at them, wondering what was wrong. Then I saw that the lenses had a pinkish shade.

I picked them up, noticing that the lenses had been replaced by the kind in the triangular pair I had found there the night before.

Just then, Helen came into the room and I could tell, even before she spoke, that she had been waiting for me.

"Joe Adams," she demanded, "what have you been up to?"

"Not a thing," I told her.

"Marge says you got Lewis all upset."

"It doesn't take a lot to upset him."

"There's something going on," she insisted, "and I want to know what it is."

I knew I was licked. "I've been trading."

"Trading! After all I've said about Bill!"

"But this is different."

"Trading is trading," she said flatly.

Bill came in the front door, but he must have heard his mother say "trading," for he ducked out again. I yelled for him to come back.

"I want both of you to sit down and listen to me," I said. "You can ask questions and offer suggestions and give me hell after I'm through."

So we sat down, all three of us, and had a family pow-wow.

It took quite a bit to make Helen believe what I had to tell, but I pointed out the dot in the desk and showed them the triangular glasses and the pair of glasses that had been refitted with the pink lenses and sent back to me. By that time, she was ready to admit there was something going on. Even so, she was fairly well burned up at me for marking up the floor around the desk legs.

I didn't show either her or Bill the pen that was a fishing rod, for I was scared of that. Flourish it around a bit and there was no telling what would happen.

Bill was interested and excited, of course. This was trading, which was right down his alley.

I cautioned both of them not to say a word about it. Bill wouldn't, for he was hell on secrets and special codes. But bright and early in the morning, Helen would probably swear Marge to secrecy, then tell her all about it and there wasn't a thing that I could do or say to stop her.

Bill wanted to put the pink-lensed spectacles on right away, to see how they were different from any other kind. I wouldn't let him. I wanted to put those specs on myself, but I was afraid to, if you want to know the truth.

When Helen went out to the kitchen to get dinner, Bill and I held a strategy session. For a ten-year-old, Bill had a lot of good ideas. We agreed that we ought to get some system into the trading, because, as Bill pointed out, the idea of swapping sight unseen was a risky sort of business. A fellow ought to have some say in what he was getting in return.

But to arrive at an understanding with whoever we were trading with meant that we'd have to set up some sort of communication system. And how do you communicate with someone you don't know the first thing about, except that perhaps it has three eyes?

Then Bill hit upon what seemed a right idea. What we needed, he said, was a catalogue. If you were going to trade with someone, the logical first step would be to let them know what you had to trade.

To be worth anything in such a circumstance, it would have to be an illustrated catalogue. And even then it might be worthless, for how could we be sure that the Trader on the other side of the desk would know what a picture was? Maybe he'd never seen a picture before. Maybe he was differently—not so much physically, although that was possible, too, but from a different viewpoint and with totally alien concepts.

But it was the only thing we had to go on, so we settled down to work up a catalogue. Bill thought we should draw one, but neither of us was any good at drawing. I suggested illustrations from magazines. But that wasn't too hot an idea, either, for pictures of items in the magazine ads are usually all prettied up, designed to catch the eye.

Then Bill had a top-notch idea. "You know that kid dictionary Aunt Ethel gave me? Why don't we send that to them? It's got a lot of pictures and not much reading in it, and that's important. The reading might confuse them."

So we went into his room and started looking through all the junk he had, searching for the dictionary. But we ran across one of the old ABC books he'd had when he was just a toddler and decided it was even better than the dictionary. It had good clear pictures and almost no reading at all. You know the kind of book I mean—A for apple, B for ball and so forth.

We took the book into the den and put it on the desk, centering it on the dot, then went out to dinner.

In the morning the book had disappeared and that was a little odd. Up until then, nothing had disappeared from the desk until late in the day.

Early that afternoon, Lewis called me up. "I'm coming down to see you, Joe. Is there a bar handy where the two of us can be alone?"

I told him there was one only a block from me and said I'd meet him there.

I got a few things cleared away, then left the office, figuring I'd go over to the bar and have a quick one before Lewis showed up.

I don't know how he did it, but he was there ahead of me, back in a corner booth. He must have broken every traffic regulation on the books.

He had a couple of drinks waiting for us and was all huddled over, like a conspirator. He was a bit out of breath, as he had every right to be.

"Marge told me," he said.

"I suspected she would."

"There could be a mint in it, Joe!"

"That's what I thought, too. That's why I'm willing to give you ten percent. . ."

"Now look here," squawked Lewis. "You can't pull a

deal like that. I wouldn't touch it for less than fifty."

"I'm letting you in on it," I said, "because you're a neighbor. I don't know beans about this technical business. I'm getting stuff I don't understand and I need some help to find out what it is, but I can always go to someone else. . ."

It took us three drinks to get the details settled—35 percent for him, 65 for me.

"Now that that's settled," I said, "suppose you tell me what you found."

"Found?"

"That block I gave you. You wouldn't have torn down here and had the drinks all set up and waiting if you hadn't found something."

"Well, as a matter of fact. . ."

"Now just a minute," I warned him. "We're going to put this in the contract—any failure to provide full and complete analysis. . ."

"What contract?"

"We're going to have a contract drawn up, so either of us can sue the other within an inch of his life for breaking it."

Which is a hell of a way to start out a business venture, but it's the only way to handle a slippery little skate like Lewis.

So he told me what he'd found. "It's an emotions gauge. That's awkward terminology, I know, but it's the best I can think of."

"What does it do?"

"It tells how happy you are or how sad or how much you hate someone."

"Oh, great," I said, disappointed. "What good is a thing like that? I don't need a gauge to tell me if I'm sore or glad or anything."

He waxed practically eloquent. "Don't you see what an instrument like that would mean to psychiatrists? It would tell more about patients than they'd ever be willing to tell about themselves. It could be used in mental institutions and it might be important in gauging reactions for the entertainment business, politics, law enforcement and Lord knows what else."

"No kidding! Then let's start marketing!"

"The only thing is. . ."

"Yes?"

"We can't manufacture them," he said frustratedly. "We haven't got the materials and we don't know how they're made. You'll have to trade for them."

"I can't. Not right away, that is. First I've got to be able to make the Traders understand what I want, and then I'll have to find out what they're willing to trade them for."

"You have some other stuff?"

"A few things."

"You better turn them over to me."

"Some that could be dangerous. Anyhow, it all belongs to me. I'll give you what I want, when I want and. . ."

We were off again.

We finally wound up by adjourning to an attorney's office. We wrote up a contract that is probably one of the legal curiosities of all time.

I'm convinced the attorney thought, and still thinks, both of us are crazy, but that's the least of my worries now.

The contract said I was to turn over to Lewis, for his determination of its technical and merchandisable nature, at least 90 percent of certain items, the source of which I alone controlled, and with the further understanding the said source was to remain at all times under my exclusive control. The other 10 percent might, without prejudice, be withheld from his examination, with the party of the first part having sole authority to make determination of which items should constitute the withheld 10 percent.

Upon the 90 percent of the items supplied him, the

party of the second part was to make a detailed analysis, in writing, accompanied by such explanatory material as was necessary to the complete understanding of the party of the first part, within no more than three months after receipt, at the end of which time the items reverted solely to the ownership of the party of the first part. Except that such a period of examination and determination might be extended, under a mutual agreement made in writing, for any stated time.

Under no circumstances should the party of the second part conceal from the party of the first part any findings he might have made upon any of the items covered by the agreement, and that such concealment, should it occur, should be considered sufficient cause for action for the recovery of damages. That under certain conditions where some of the items might be found to be manufacturable, they could be manufactured under the terms of clauses A, B and C, section XII of this agreement.

Provisions for a sales organization to market any of said items shall be set up and made a part of this agreement. That any proceeds from such sales shall be divided as follows: 65 percent to the party of the first part (me, in case you've gotten lost, which is understandable), and 35 percent to the party of the second part (Lewis); costs to be apportioned accordingly.

There were a lot more details, of course, but that gives you an idea.

We got home from the attorney's office, without either of us knifing the other, and found Marge over at my place. Lewis went in with me to have a look at the desk.

Apparently the Trader had received the ABC book all right and had been able to understand why it was sent, for there, lying on the desk, was a picture cut out of the book. Well, not cut out, exactly—it looked more as though it had been burned out.

The picture on the desk was Z for zebra.

Lewis stared worriedly at it. "Now we're really in a

fix."

"Yeah," I admitted. "I don't know what the market price is, but they can't be cheap."

"Figure it out—expedition, safari, cages, ship, rail, fodder, keeper. You think we can switch him to something else?"

"I don't see how. He's put in his order."

Bill came wandering in and wanted to know what was up. When I glumly told him, he said cheerfully, "Aw, that's the whole trick in trading, Pop. If you got a bum jackknife you want to trade, you unload it on somebody who doesn't know what a good knife is like."

Lewis didn't get it, but I did. "That's right! He doesn't know a zebra is an animal, or, if he does, how big it is!"

"Sure," Bill said confidently. "All he saw was a picture."

It was five o'clock then, but the three of us went uptown and shopped. Bill found a cheap bracelet charm about the size of the drawing in the book. When it comes to junk like that, my kid knows just where it's sold and how much it costs. I considered making him a junior partner in charge of such emergencies, with about 10 percent share or so—out of Lewis's 35 percent, of course—but I was sure Lewis wouldn't hold still for that. I decided instead to give Bill a dollar a week allowance, said compensation to commence immediately upon our showing a profit.

Well, we had Z for zebra—provided the Trader was satisfied with a little piece of costume jewelry. It was lucky, I thought, that it hadn't been Z for zephyr.

The rest of the alphabet was easy, yet I couldn't help but kick myself over all the time we were wasting. Of all the unworthy catalogues we might have sent, that ABC book was the worst. But until the Trader had run through the whole list, I was afraid to send another for fear of confusing him.

So I sent him an apple and a ball and a small doll for a girl and toy cat and toy dog, and so on, and then I lay awake nights wondering what the Trader would make of them. I could picture him trying to learn the use of a rubber doll or cat.

I'd given Lewis the two pairs of glasses, but had held back the fountain-pen fishing rod, for I was still scared of that one. He had turned over the emotion gauge to a psychiatrist to try out in his practice as a sort of field test.

Marge and Helen, knowing that Lewis and I had entered into some kind of partnership, were practically inseparable now. Helen kept telling me how glad she was that I had finally recognized what a sterling fellow Lewis was. I suppose Lewis heard the same thing about me from Marge.

Bill went around practically busting to do some bragging. But Bill is a great little businessman and he kept his mouth shut. I told him about the allowance, of course.

Lewis was all for trying to ask the Trader for a few more of the emotion gauges. He had a draftsman at the plant draw up a picture of the gauge and he wanted me to send it through to indicate that we were interested in it.

But I told him not to try to rush things. While the emotion gauge might be a good deal, we should sample what the Trader had to offer before we made up our minds.

The Trader, apparently certain now that someone was cooperating with him, had dropped his once-a-day trade schedule and was open for business around the clock. After he had run through the list in the ABC book, he sent back a couple of blank pages from the book with very crude drawings on them—drawings that looked as if they had been made with crumbly charcoal. Lewis drew a series of pictures, showing how a pencil worked, and we sent the Trader a ream of paper and a gross of sharpened pencils, then sat back to wait.

We waited a week and were getting sort of edgy, when back came the entire ream of paper, with each sheet covered on both sides with all kinds of drawings. So we sent him a mail-order catalogue, figuring that would hold him for a while, and settled down to try to puzzle out the drawings he had made.

There wasn't a single thing that made any sense at all—not even to Lewis. He'd study some of the drawings, then pace up and down the room, pulling his hair and twitching his ears. Then he'd study the drawings some more.

To me, it all looked plain Rube Goldbergish.

Finally, we figured we might as well forget about the catalogue idea, for the time being at least, and we started feeding all sorts of stuff through the desk—scissors, dishes, shoes, jackknives, mucilage, cigars, paper clips, erasers, spoons—almost anything that was handy. It wasn't the scientific way, I know, but we didn't have the time to get very methodical about it and, until we had a chance to work out a more sensible program, we figured we might as well try the shotgun method.

And the Trader started shooting things back at us. We'd sit for hours and feed stuff through to him and then he'd shoot stuff back at us and we had the damnedest pile of junk heaped all over the place you ever laid eyes on.

We rigged up a movie camera and took a lot of film of the spot on the desk where the exchange was going on. We spent a lot of time viewing that film, slowing it down and even stopping it, but it didn't tell us anything at all. When the stuff disappeared or appeared, it just disappeared or appeared. One frame it would be there, the next frame it would be gone.

Lewis canceled all his other work and used the lab for nothing but trying to puzzle out the gadgets that we got. Most of them we couldn't crack at all. I imagine they were useful in some way, but we never managed to learn how.

There was the perfume bottle, for example. That is what we called it, anyhow. But there was a suspicion in our minds that the perfume was simply a secondary effect, that the so-called bottle was designed for some other purpose entirely.

Lewis and his boys were studying it down at the lab trying to make out some rhyme or reason for it, and somehow they turned it on. They worked for three days, the last two in gas masks, trying to turn it off again. When the smell got so bad that people began calling the police, we took the contraption out into the country and buried it. Within a few days, all the vegetation in the area was dead. All the rest of the summer, the boys from the agricultural department at the university ran around, practically frothing at the mouth, trying to find the cause.

There was the thing that might have been a clock of some sort, although it might just as easily have been something else. If it was a clock, the Trader had a time system that would drive you nuts, for it would measure the minutes or hours or whatever they were like lightning for a while, then barely move for an entire day.

And there was the one you'd point at something and press a certain spot on it—not a button or a knob or anything as crass and mechanical as that, just a certain spot—and there'd be just a big blank spot in the landscape. But when you stopped pressing, the landscape would come back again, unchanged. We filed it away in the darkest corner of the laboratory safe, with a big red tag on it marked: *Dangerous! Don't Monkey with This!*

But most of the items we just drew blanks on. And it kept coming all the time. I piled the garage full of it and started dumping it in the basement. Some of it I was scared of and hauled out to the dump.

In the meantime, Lewis was having trouble with the emotion gauge. "It works," he said. "The psychiatrist I gave it to to try out is enthusiastic about it. But it seems almost impossible to get it on the market."

"If it works," I objected, handing him a can of beer, "it ought to sell."

"In any other field, it might, but you don't handle merchandise that way in the medical field. Before you can put something on the market, you have to have it nailed down with blueprints and theory and field tests and such. And we can't. We don't know *how* it works. We don't know *why* it works. Until we do, no reputable medical supply house will take it on, no approved medical journal will advertise it, no practitioner will use it."

"Then I guess it's out." I felt fairly blue about it, because it was the only thing we had that we knew how to use. Lewis nodded and drank his beer and was glummer than ever.

Looking back on it, it's funny how we found the gadget that made us all the money. Actually, it wasn't Lewis but Helen who found it.

Helen is a good housewife. She's always going after things with the vacuum and the dustcloth and she washes the woodwork so often and so furiously that we have to paint it every year.

One night, we were sitting in the living room, watching television.

"Joe," she asked me, "did you dust the den?"

"Dust the den? What would I want to do that for?"

"Well, someone did. Maybe it was Bill."

"Bill wouldn't be caught dead with a dustcloth in his mitt."

"I can't understand it, Joe," she said. "I went in there to dust it and it was absolutely clean. Everything just shone."

Sgt. Friday was trying to get the facts out of someone and his sidekick was complaining about some relatives that had come to visit and I didn't pay much attention at the time.

But the next day, I got to thinking about it and I couldn't get it off my mind. I certainly hadn't dusted the den and it was a cinch Bill hadn't, yet someone had if Helen was ready to admit it was clean.

So, that evening, I went out into the street with a pail and shoveled up a pailful of dirt and brought it in the house.

Helen caught me as I was coming in the door. "What do you think you're doing with that?"

"Experimenting," I told her.

"Do it in the garage."

"It isn't possible," I argued. "I have to find out who's been dusting the den."

I knew that, if my hunch failed, I'd have a lot to answer for when she followed me and stood in the doorway, ready to pounce.

There was a bunch of junk from the Trader standing on the desk and a lot more of it in one corner. I cleared off the desk and that was when Bill came in.

"What are you doing, Dad?" he asked.

"Your father's gone insane," Helen explained quietly.

They stood there, watching me, while I took a handful of dirt and sprinkled on the desk top.

It stayed there for just an instant—and then it was gone. The top of the desk was spotless.

"Bill," I said, "take one of those gadgets out to the garage."

"Which one?"

"It doesn't matter."

So he took one and I spread another handful of dirt and, in a second, it was gone.

Bill was back by that time and I sent him out with another gadget.

We kept on like that for quite a while and Bill was beginning to get disgusted with me. But finally I sprinkled the dirt and it stayed.

"Bill," I said, "you remember the last thing you took out?"

"Sure."

"Well, go out and bring it back again."

He got it and, as soon as he reached the door of the

den, the dirt disappeared.

"Well, that's it," I said.

"That's what?" asked Helen.

I pointed to the contraption Bill had in his hand. "That. Throw away your vacuum cleaner. Burn up the dustcloth. Heave out the mop. Just have one of those in the house and. . ."

She threw herself into my arms.

"Oh, *Joe!*"

We danced a jig, the two of us.

Then I sat around for a while, kicking myself for tying up with Lewis, wondering if maybe there wasn't some way I could break the contract now that I had found something without any help from him. But I remembered all those clauses he had written in. It wouldn't have been any use, anyhow, for Helen was already across the street, telling Marge about it.

So I phoned Lewis at the lab and he came tearing over.

We ran field tests.

The living room was spotless from Bill just having walked through it, carrying the gadget, and the garage, where he had taken it momentarily, was spic and span. While we didn't check it, I imagine that an area paralleling the path he had taken from the front door to the garage was the only place outdoors that didn't have a speck of dust upon it.

We took the gadget down in the basement and cleaned that up. We sneaked over to a neighbor's back yard, where we knew there was a lot of cement dust, held the gadget over it and in an instant there wasn't any cement dust. There were just a few pebbles left and the pebbles, I suppose, you couldn't rightly classify as dust.

We didn't need to know any more.

Back at the house, I broke open a bottle of Scotch I'd been saving, while Lewis sat down at the kitchen table and drew a sketch of the gadget.

We had a drink, then went into the den and put the

drawing on the desk. The drawing disappeared and we waited. In a few minutes, another one of the gadgets appeared. We waited for a while and nothing happened.

"We've got to let him know we want a lot of them," I said.

"There's no way we can," said Lewis. "We don't know his mathematical symbols, he doesn't know ours, and there's no surefire way to teach him. He doesn't know a single word of our language and we don't know a word of his."

We went back to the kitchen and had another drink.

Lewis sat down and drew a row of the gadgets across a sheet of paper, then sketched in representations of others behind them so that, when you looked at it, you could see that there were hundreds of them.

We sent that through.

Fourteen gadgets came back—the exact number Lewis had sketched in the first row.

Apparently the Trader had no idea of perspective. The lines that Lewis had drawn to represent the other gadgets behind the first row didn't mean a thing to him.

We went back to the kitchen and had a few more drinks.

"We'll need thousands of the things," said Lewis, holding his head in his hands. "I can't sit here day and night, drawing them."

"You may have to do that," I said, enjoying myself.

"There *must* be another way."

"Why not draw a bunch of them, then mimeograph the drawing?" I suggested. "We could send the mimeograph sheets through to him in bundles."

I hated to say it, because I was still enamored of the idea of sticking Lewis somewhere off in a corner, sentenced to a lifetime of drawing the same thing over and over.

"That might work," said Lewis, brightening annoyingly. "It's just simple enough. . ."

"Practical is the word," I snapped. "If it were simple, you'd have thought of it."

"I leave things like that to detail men."

"You'd better!"

It took a while and a whole bottle before we calmed down.

Next day, we bought a mimeograph machine and Lewis drew a stencil with twenty-five of the gadgets on it. We ran through a hundred sheets and sent them through the desk.

It worked—we were busy for several hours, getting those gadgets out of the way as they poured through to use.

I'm afraid we never stopped to think about what the Trader might want in return for the dust-collectors. We were so excited that we forgot, for the moment, that this was a commercial proposition and not just something gratis.

But the next afternoon, back came the mimeographed sheets we'd sent through and, on the reverse side of each of them, the Trader had drawn twenty-five representations of the zebra bracelet charm.

And there we were, faced with the necessity of getting together pronto, twenty-five hundred of those silly zebras.

I tore down to the store where I'd gotten the bracelet, but all they had in stock were two dozen of the things. They said they didn't think they could order any more. The number, they said, had been discontinued.

The name of the company that made them was stamped on the inside of the bracelet and, as soon as I got home, I put in a long distance call.

I finally got hold of the production manager. "You know those bracelets you put out?"

"We put out millions of 'em. Which one are you talking about?"

"The one with the zebra on it."

He thought a moment. "Yeah, we did. Quite a while ago. We don't make them any more. In this business. . ."

"I need at least twenty-five hundred of them."

"Twenty-five hundred bracelets?"

"No, just the zebras."

"Look, is this a gag?"

"It's no gag, mister," I said. "I need those zebras. I'm willing to pay for them."

"We haven't any in stock."

"Couldn't you make them?"

"Not just twenty-five hundred of them. Wouldn't be worth it to put through a special order for so few. If it was fifty thousand, say, we might consider it."

"All right, then," I said. "How much for fifty thousand?"

He named a price and we haggled some, but I was in no position to do much bargaining. We finally agreed on a price I knew was way too high, considering the fact that the entire bracelet, with the zebra and a lot of other junk, had only retailed at 39 cents.

"And hold the order open," I told him. "We might want more of them."

"Okay," he said. "Just one thing—would you mind telling me what you want with fifty thousand zebras?"

"Yes, I would," I said and hung up.

I suppose he thought I was off my rocker, but who cared what he thought?

It took ten days to get that shipment of fifty thousand zebras and I sweated out every minute of it. Then there was the job of getting them under cover when it came and, in case you don't know, fifty thousand zebras, even when they're only bracelet charms, take up room.

But first I took out twenty-five hundred and sent them through the desk.

For the ten days since we'd gotten the dust-collectors, we'd sent nothing through and there had been no sign from the Trader that he might be getting impatient. I wouldn't have blamed him a bit if he'd done something, like sending through his equivalent of a bomb, to express his dissatisfaction at our slow delivery. I've often wondered what he thought of the long delay—if he hadn't suspected we were reneging on the bargain.

All this time, I had been smoking too much and gnawing my fingernails and I'd figured that Lewis was just as busy seeing what could be done about marketing the dusters.

But when I mentioned it to him he just looked blank.

"You know, Joe, I've been doing a lot of worrying."

"We haven't a thing to worry about now," I said, "except getting these things sold."

"But the dust must go somewhere," he fretted.

"The dust?"

"Sure, the dust these things collect. Remember we picked up an entire pile of cement dust? What I want to know is where it all went. The gadget itself isn't big enough to hold it. It isn't big enough to hold even a week's collection of dust from the average house. That's what worries me—where does it go?"

"I don't care where. It goes, doesn't it?"

"That's the pragmatic view," he said scornfully.

It turned out that Lewis hadn't done a thing about marketing, so I got busy.

But I ran into the same trouble we'd had trying to sell the emotion gauge.

The dust collector wasn't patented and it didn't have a brand name. There was no fancy label stuck on it and it didn't bear a manufacturer's imprint. And when anybody asked me how it worked, I couldn't answer.

One wholesaler did make me a ridiculous offer. I laughed in his face and walked out.

That night, Lewis and I sat around the kitchen table, drinking beer, and neither of us too happy. I could see a lot of trouble ahead in getting the gadgets sold. Lewis, it seemed, was still worrying about what happened to the dust.

He had taken one of the dust collectors apart and the only thing he could find out about it was that there was some feeble force-field operating inside of it—feeble yet strong enough to play hell with the electrical circuits and fancy metering machinery he has at the lab. As soon as he found out what was happening, he slapped the cover back on as quick as he could and then everything was all right. The cover was a shield against the force-field.

"That dust must be getting thrown into another dimension," he told me, looking like a hound dog that had lost a coon track.

"Maybe not. It could be winding up in one of those dust clouds way out in space."

He shook his head.

"You can't tell me," I said, "that the Trader is crazy enough to sell us a gadget that will throw dust back into his face."

"You miss the point entirely. The Trader is operating from another dimension. He *must* be. And if there are two dimensions, his and ours, there may be others. The Trader must have used these dust collectors himself—not for the same purpose we intend, perhaps, but they get rid of something that he doesn't want around. So, necessarily, they'd have to be rigged to get rid of it in a dimension other than his."

We sat there drinking beer and I started turning over that business about different dimensions in my head. I couldn't grasp the concept. Maybe Lewis was right about me being a pragmatist. If you can't see it or touch it or even guess what it would be like, how can you believe there might be another dimension? I couldn't.

So I started to talk about marketing the dust collector and before Lewis went home that night, we'd decided that the only thing left to do was sell it door to door. We even agreed to charge $12.50 for it. The zebras figured out to four cents each and we would pay our salesmen ten percent commission, which would leave us a profit of $11.21 apiece.

I put an ad in the paper for salesmen and the next day we had several applicants. We started them out on a trial run.

Those gadgets sold like hotcakes and we knew we were in!

I quit my job and settled down to handling the sales end, while Lewis went back to the lab and started going through the pile of junk he had gotten from the Trader.

There are a lot of headaches running a sales campaign. You have to map out territories for your salemen, get clearance from Better Business Bureaus, bail out your men if they're thrown in the clink for running afoul of some obscure village ordinance. There are more worrisome angles to it than you can ever imagine.

But in a couple of months' time, things were running pretty smoothly. We had the state well covered and were branching out into others. I had ordered another fifty thousand zebras and told them to expect re-orders—and the desk top was a busy place. It got to a point, finally, where I had to hire three men full time, paying them plenty not to talk, to man the desk top twenty-four hours a day. We'd send through zebras for eight hours, then take away dust gadgets for eight hours, then feed through zebras for another eight.

If the Trader had an qualms about what was happening, he gave no sing of it. He seemed perfectly happy to send us dust collectors so long as we sent him zebras.

The neighbors were curious and somewhat upset at first, but finally they got used to it. If I could have moved to some other location, I would have, for the house was more an office than a home and we had practically no family life at all. But if we wanted to stay in business, we had to stay right where we were because it was the only place we had contact with the Trader.

The money kept rolling in and I turned the management of it over to Helen and Marge. The income tax boys gave us a rough time when we didn't show any manufacturing expenses, but since we weren't inclined to argue over what we had to pay, they couldn't do anything about it.

Lewis was wearing himself down to a nubbin at the lab, but he wasn't finding anything that we could use.

But he still did some worrying now and then about where all that dust was going. And he was right, probably for the first time in his life.

One afternoon, a couple of years after we'd started selling the dust collectors, I had been uptown to attend to some banking difficulties that Helen and Marge had gotten all bollixed up. I'd no more than pulled into the driveway when Helen came busting out of the house. She was covered with dust, her face streaked with it, and she was the maddest-looking woman I have ever seen.

"You've got to do something about it, Joe!" she shrieked.

"About what?"

"The dust! It's pouring into the house!"

"Where is it pouring from?"

"From *everywhere!*"

I could see she'd opened all the windows and there was dust pouring out of them, almost like a smoke cloud. I got out of the car and took a quick look up and down the street. Every house in the block had its windows open and there was dust coming out of all of them and the neighborhood was boiling with angry, screaming women.

"Where's Bill?" I asked.

"Out back."

I ran around the house and called him and he came running. Marge had come across the street and, if anything, she was about six degrees sorer about all the dust than Helen was.

"Get in the car," I said.

"Where are we going?" Marge demanded.

"Out to pick up Lewis."

I must have sounded like nothing to trifle with, for they piled in and I got out of there as fast as the car would take us.

The homes and factories and stores that had bought the gadget were gushing so much dust, visibility wouldn't be worth a damn before long.

I had to wade through about two feet of dust on the laboratory floor to get to Lewis's office and hold a handkerchief over my nose to keep from suffocating.

Inside the car we got our faces wiped off and most of the dust hacked out of our throats. I could see then that Lewis was about three shades paler than usual, although to tell the truth, he always was a pasty-looking creature.

"It's the creatures from the third dimension," he said anxiously. "The place where we were sending all the dust. They got sick and tired of having it pour in on them and they got it figured out and now they're firing the dust right back at us."

"Now calm down. We're just jumping at the conclusion that this was caused by our gadget."

"I checked, Joe. It was. The dust is coming out in jets from every single place where we sent it through. No place else."

"Then all we have to do is fire it back at them."

He shook his head. "Not a chance. The gadget works one way now—from them to us." He coughed and looked wildly at me. "Think of it! A couple of million homes, stores and factories—some of them operating for two whole years! Joe, what are we going to do?"

"We're going to hole up somewhere till this—well, blows over."

Being of a nasty legal turn of mind, he probably foresaw even then the countless lawsuits that would avalanche on us. Personally, I was more scared of being mobbed by angry women.

But that's all past history. We hid out till people had quieted down and then began trying to settle the suits out of court. We had a lot of money and were able to pay off most of them. The judgments against us still outstanding don't amount to more than a few hundred thousand. We could wipe that out pretty quickly if we'd just hit on something else as profitable as the cleaning gadget.

Lewis is working hard at it, but he isn't having any luck. And the Trader is gone now. As soon as we dared come home, I went into the house and had a look at the desk. The inlaid dot was gone. I tried putting something where it had been, but nothing happened.

What scared the Trader off? I'd give a lot to know. Meanwhile, there are some commercial prospects.

The rose-tinted glasses, for instance, that we call the Happiness Lenses. Put them on and you're happy as a clam. Almost every person on the face of the Earth would like a pair of them, so they could forget their troubles for a while. They would probably play hob with the liquor business.

The trouble is that we don't know how to make them and, now that the Trader's gone, we can't swap for them.

But there's one thing that keeps worrying me. I know I shouldn't let it bother me, but I can't keep it out of mind.

Just what did the Trader do with those couple of million zebras we sent him?

Neighbor

Coon Valley is a pleasant place, but there's no denying it's sort of off the beaten track and it's not a place where you can count on getting rich because the farms are small and a lot of the ground is rough. You can farm the bottomlands, but the hillsides are only good for pasture and the roads are just dirt roads, impassable at certain times of year.

The old-timers, like Bert Smith and Jingo Harris and myself, are well satisfied to stay here, for we grew up with the country and we haven't any illusions about getting rich and we'd feel strange and out-of-place anywhere but in the valley. But there are others, newcomers, who move in and get discouraged after a while and up and move away, so there usually is a farm or two standing idle, waiting to be sold.

We are just plain dirt farmers, with emphasis on the dirt, for we can't afford a lot of fancy machinery and we don't go in for blooded stock—but there's nothing wrong with us; we're just everyday, the kind of people you meet all over the United States. Because we're out of the way and some of the families have lived here for so long, I suppose you could say that we have gotten clannish. But that doesn't mean we don't like outside folks; it just means we've lived so long together that we've got to know and like one another and are satisfied with things just as they are.

We have radios, of course, and we listen to the programs and the news, and some of us take daily papers, but I'm afraid that we may be a bit provincial, for it's fairly hard to get us stirred up much about world happenings. There's so much of interest right here in the valley we haven't got the time to worry about all those outside things. I imagine you'd call us conservative, for most of us vote Republican without even wondering why and there's none of us who has much time for all this government interference in the farming business.

The valley has always been a pleasant place—not only the land, but the people in it, and we've always been fortunate in the new neighbors that we get. Despite new ones coming in every year or so, we've never had a really bad one and that means a lot to us.

But we always worry a little when one of the new ones up and moves away and we speculate among ourselves, wondering what kind of people will buy or rent the vacant farm.

The old Lewis farm had been abandoned for a long time, the buildings all run down and gone to ruin and the fields gone back to grass. A dentist over at Hopkins Corners had rented it for several years and run some cattle in it, driving out on weekends to see how they were doing. We used to wonder every now and then if anyone would ever farm the place again, but finally we quit wondering, for the buildings had fallen into such disrepair that we figured no one ever would. I went in one day and talked to the banker at Hopkins Corners, who had the renting of the place, and told him I'd like to take it over if the dentist ever gave it up. But he told me the owners, who lived in Chicago then, were anxious to sell rather than to rent it, although he didn't seem too optimistic that anyone would buy it.

Then one spring a new family moved onto the farm and in time we learned it had been sold and that the new family's name was Heath—Reginald Heath. And Bert Smith said to me: "Reginald! That's a hell of a name for a farmer!" But that was all he said.

Jingo Harris stopped by one day, coming home from town, when he saw Heath out in the yard, to pass the time of day. It was a neighborly thing to do, of course, and Heath seemed glad to have him stop, although Jingo said he seemed to be a funny kind of man to be a farmer.

"He's a foreigner," Jingo told me. "Sort of dark. Like he might be a Spaniard or from one of those other countries. I don't know how he got that Reginald. Reginald is English and Heath's no Englishman."

Later on we heard that the Heaths weren't really Spanish, but were Rumanians or Bulgarians and that they were refugees from the Iron Curtain.

But Spanish, or Rumanian, or Bulgarian, the Heaths were workers. There was Heath and his wife and a half-grown girl and all three of them worked all the blessed time. They paid attention to their business and didn't bother anyone and because of this we liked them, although we didn't have much to do with them. Not that we didn't want to or that they didn't want us to; it's just that in a community like ours new folks sort of have to grow in instead of being taken in.

Heath had an old beaten-up wired-together tractor that made a lot of noise, and as soon as the soil was dry enough to plow he started out to turn over the fields that through the years had grown up to grass. I used to wonder if he worked all night long, for many times when I went to bed I heard the tractor running. Although that may not be as late as it sounds to city dwellers, for here in the valley we go to bed early—and get up early, too.

One night after dark I set out to hunt some cows, a couple of fence-jumping heifers that gave me lots of trouble. Just let a man come in late from work and tired and maybe it's raining a little and dark as the inside of a cat and those two heifers would turn up missing and I'd have to go and hunt them. I tried all the different kinds of pokes and none of them did any good. When a heifer gets to fence-jumping there isn't much that can be done with her.

So I lit a lantern and set out to hunt for them, but I hunted for two hours and didn't find a trace of them. I had just about decided to give up and go back home when I heard the sound of a tractor running and realized that I was just above the west field of the old Lewis place. To get home I'd have to go right past the field and I figured it might be as well to wait when I reached the field until the tractor came around and ask Heath if he had seen the heifers.

It was a dark night, with thin clouds hiding the stars and a wind blowing high in the treetops and there was a smell of rain in the air. Heath, I figured, probably was staying out extra late to finish up the field ahead of the coming rain, although I remember that I thought he was pushing things just a little hard. Already he was far ahead of all the others in the valley with his plowing.

So I made my way down the steep hillside and waded the creek at a shallow place I knew and while I was doing this I heard the tractor make a complete round of the field. I looked for the headlight, but I didn't see it and I thought probably the trees had hidden it from me.

I reached the edge of the field and climbed through the fence, walking out across the furrows to intercept the tractor. I heard it make the turn to the east of me and start down the field toward me and although I could hear the noise of it, there wasn't any light.

I found the last furrow and stood there waiting, sort of wondering, not too alarmed as yet, how Heath managed to drive the rig without any light. I thought that maybe he had cat eyes and could see in the dark and although it seemed funny later when I remembered it, the idea that a man might have cat eyes did not seem funny then.

The noise kept getting louder and it seemed to be coming pretty close, when all at once the tractor rushed out of the dark and seemed to leap at me. I guess I must have been afraid that it would run over me, for I jumped back a yard or two, with my heart up in my neck. But I needn't have bothered, for I was out of the way to start with.

The tractor went on past me and I waved the lantern and yelled for Heath to stop and as I waved the lantern the light was thrown onto the rear of the tractor and I saw there was no one on it.

A hundred things went through my mind, but the one idea that stuck was that Heath had fallen off the tractor and might be lying injured, somewhere in the field.

I ran after the tractor, thinking to shut it down before it got loose and ran into a tree or something, but by the time I reached it, it had reached a turn and it was making that turn as neatly as if it had been broad daylight and someone had been driving it.

I jumped up on the drawbar and grabbed the seat, hauling myself up. I reached out a hand, grabbing for the throttle, but with my hand upon the metal I didn't pull it back. The tractor had completed the turn now and was going down the furrow—and there was something else.

Take an old tractor, now—one that wheezed and coughed and hammered and kept threatening to fall apart, like this one did—and you are bound to get a lot of engine vibration. But in this tractor there was no vibration. It ran along as smooth as a high-priced car and the only jolts you got were when the wheels hit a bump or slight gully in the field.

I stood there, hanging onto the lantern with one hand and clutching the throttle with the other, and I didn't do a thing. I just rode down to the point where the tractor started to make another turn. Then I stepped off and went on home. I didn't hunt for Heath lying in the field, for I knew he wasn't there.

I suppose I wondered how it was possible, but I didn't really fret myself too much trying to figure it all out. I imagine, in the first place, I was just too numb. You may worry a lot about little things that don't seem quite right, but when you run into a big thing, like that self-operating tractor, you sort of give up automatically, knowing that it's too big for your brain to handle, that it's something you haven't got a chance of solving. And after a while you forget it because it's something you can't live with. So your mind rejects it.

I got home and stood out in the barnyard for a moment, listening. The wind was blowing fairly hard by then and the first drops of rain were falling, but every now and then, when the wind would quiet down, I could hear the tractor.

I went inside the house and Helen and the kids were all in bed and sound asleep, so I didn't say anything about it that night. And the next morning, when I had a chance to think about it, I didn't say anything at all. Mostly, I suppose, because I knew no one would believe me and that I'd have to take a lot of kidding about automatic tractors.

Heath got his plowing done and his crops in, well ahead of everyone in the valley. The crops came up in good shape and we had good growing weather; then along in June we got a spell of wet, and everyone got behind with corn plowing because you can't go out in the field when the ground is soggy. All of us chored around our places, fixing fences and doing other odd jobs, cussing out the rain and watching the weeds grow like mad in the unplowed field.

All of us, that is, except Heath. His corn was clean as a whistle and you had to hunt to find a weed. Jingo stopped by one day and asked him how he managed, but Heath just laughed a little, in that quiet way of his, and talked of something else.

The first apples finally were big enough for green-apple pies and there is no one in the country makes better green-apple pies than Helen. She wins prizes with her pies every year at the county fair and she is proud of them.

One day she wrapped up a couple of pies and took them over to the Heaths. It's a neighborly way we have of doing in the valley, with the women running back and forth from one neighbor to another with their cooking. Each one of them has some dish she likes to show off to the neighbors and it's a sort of harmless way of bragging.

Helen and the Heaths got along just swell. She was late in getting home and I was starting supper, with the kids yelling they were hungry when-do-we-eat-around-here, when she finally showed up.

She was full of talk about the Heaths—how they had fixed up the house, you never would have thought anyone could do so much to such a terribly run-down place as they had, and about the garden they had—especially about the garden. It was a big one, she said, and beautifully taken care of and it was full of vegetables she had never seen before. The funniest things you ever saw, she said. Not the ordinary kind of vegetables.

We talked some about those vegetables, speculating that maybe the Heaths had brought the seeds out with them from behind the Iron Curtain, although so far as I could remember, vegetables were vegetables, no matter where you were. They grew the same things in Russia or Rumania or Timbuktu as we did. And, anyhow, by this time I was getting a little skeptical about that story of their escaping from Rumania.

But we didn't have the time for much serious speculation on the Heaths, although there was plenty of casual gossip going around the neighborhood. Haying came along and then the small-grain harvest and everyone was busy. The hay was good and the small-grain crop was fair, but it didn't look like we'd get much corn. For we hit a drought. That's the way it goes—too much rain in June, not enough in August.

We watched the corn and watched the sky and felt hopeful when a cloud showed up, but the clouds never meant a thing. It just seems at times that God isn't on your side.

Then one morning Jingo Harris showed up and stood around, first on one foot, then the other, talking to me while I worked on an old corn binder that was about worn out and which it didn't look nohow I'd need to use that year.

"Jingo," I said, after I'd watched him fidget for an hour or more, "you got something on your mind."

He blurted it out then. "Heath got rain last night," he said.

"No one else did," I told him.

"I guess you're right," said Jingo. "Heath's the only one."

He told me how he'd gone to cut through Heath's north cornfield, carrying back a couple of balls of binder twine he'd borrowed from Bert Smith. It wasn't until he'd crawled through the fence that he noticed the field was wet, soaked by a heavy rain.

"It must have happened in the night," he said.

He thought it was funny, but figured maybe there had been a shower across the lower end of the valley, although as a rule rains travel up and down the valley, not across it. But when he had crossed the corner of the field and crawled through the fence, he noticed it hadn't rained at all. So he went back and walked around the field and the rain had fallen on the field, but nowhere else. It began at the fence and ended at the fence.

When he'd made a circuit of the field he sat down on one of the balls of twine and tried to get it all thought out but it made no sense—furthermore, it was plain unbelievable.

Jingo is a thorough man. He likes to have all the evidence and know all there is to know before he makes up his mind. So he went over to Heath's second corn patch, on the west side of the valley. And once again, he found that it had rained on that field—on the field, but not around the field.

"What do you make of it?" Jingo asked me and I said I didn't know. I came mighty close to telling him about the unmanned tractor, but I thought better of it. After all, there was no point in getting the neighborhood stirred up.

After Jingo left I got in the car and drove over to the Heath farm, intending to ask him if he could loan me his posthole digger for a day or two. Not that I was going to dig any postholes, but you have to have some excuse for showing up at a neighbor's place.

I never got a chance to ask him for that posthole digger, though. Once I got there I never even thought of it.

Heath was sitting on the front steps of the porch and he seemed glad to see me. He came down to the car and shook my hand and said, "It's good to see you, Calvin." The way he said it made me feel friendly and sort of important, too—especially that Calvin business, for everyone else just calls me Cal. I'm not downright sure, in fact, that anyone in the neighborhood remembers that my name is Calvin.

"I'd like to show you around the place," he said. "We've done some fixing up."

Fixing up wasn't exactly the word for it. The place was spic and span. It looked like some of those Pennsylvania and Connecticut farms you see in the magazines. The house and all the other buildings had been ramshackle with all the paint peeled off them and looking as they might fall down at any minute. But now they had a sprightly, solid look and they gleamed with paint. They didn't look new, of course, but they looked as if they'd always been well taken care of and painted every year. The fences were all fixed up and painted, too, and the weeds were cut and a couple of old unsightly scrap-lumber piles had been cleaned up and burned. Heath had even tackled an old iron and machinery junk pile and had it sorted out.

"There was a lot to do," said Heath, "but I feel it's worth it. I have an orderly soul. I like to have things neat."

Which might be true, of course, but he'd done it all in less than six months' time. He'd come to the farm in early March and it was only August and he'd not only put in some hundred acres of crops and done all the other farm work, but he'd got the place fixed up. And that wasn't possible, I told myself. One man couldn't do it, not even with his wife and daughter helping—not even if he worked twenty-four hours a day and didn't stop to eat. Or unless he could take time and stretch it out to make one hour equal three or four.

I trailed along behind Heath and thought about the time-stretching business and was pleased at myself for thinking of it, for it isn't often that I get foolish thoughts that are likewise pleasing. Why, I thought, with a deal like that you could stretch out any day so you could get all the work done you wanted to. And if you could stretch out time, maybe you could compress it, too, so that a trip to a dentist, for example, would only seem to take a minute.

Heath took me out to the garden and Helen had been right. There were the familiar vegetables, of course—cabbages and tomatoes and squashes and all the other kinds that were found in every garden—but in addition to this there were as many others I had never seen before. He told me the names of them and they seemed to be queer names then, although now it seems a little strange to think they once had sounded queer, for now everyone in the valley grows these vegetables and it seems like we have always had them.

As we talked he pulled up and picked some of the

strange vegetables and put them in a basket he had brought along.

"You'll want to try them all," he said. "Some of them you may not like at first, but there are others that you will. This one you eat raw, sliced like a tomato, and this one is best boiled, although you can bake it, too—"

I wanted to ask him how he'd come on the vegetables and where they had come from, but he didn't give me a chance; he kept on telling me about them and how to cook them and that this one was a winter keeper and that one you could can and he gave me one to eat raw and it was rather good.

We'd got to the far end of the garden and were starting to come back when Heath's wife ran around the corner of the house.

Apparently she didn't see me at first or had forgotten I was there, for she called to him and the name she called him wasn't Reginald or Reggie, but a foreign-sounding name. I won't even try to approximate it, for even at the time I wasn't able to recall it a second after hearing it. It was like no word I'd ever heard before.

Then she saw me and stopped running and caught her breath, and a moment later said she'd been listening in on the party line and that Bert Smith's little daughter, Ann, was terribly sick.

"They called the doctor," she said, "but he is out on calls and he won't get there in time."

"Reginald," she said, "the symptoms sound like—"

And she said another name that was like none I'd ever heard or expect to hear again.

Watching Heath's face, I could swear I saw it pale despite his olive tinge of skin.

"Quick!" he shouted and grabbed me by the arm.

We ran around in front to his old clunk of a car. He threw the basket of vegetables in the back seat and jumped behind the wheel. I scrambled in after him and tried to close the door, but it wouldn't close. The lock kept slipping loose and I had to hang onto the door so it wouldn't bang.

We lit out of there like a turpentined dog and the noise that old car made was enough to deafen one. Despite my holding onto it, the door kept banging and all the fenders rattled and there was every other kind of noise you'd expect a junk-heap car to make, with an extra two or three thrown in.

I wanted to ask him what he planned to do, but I was having trouble framing the question in my mind and even if I had known how to phrase it I doubt he could have heard me with all the racket that the car was making.

So I hung on as best I could and tried to keep the door from banging and all at once it seemed to me the car was making more noise than it had any call to. Just like the old haywire tractor made more noise than any tractor should. Too much noise, by far, for the way that it was running. Just like on the tractor, there was no engine vibration and despite all the banging and the clanking we were making time. As I've said, our valley roads are none too good, but even so I swear there were places we hit seventy and we went around sharp corners where, by rights, we should have gone into the ditch at the speed that we were going, but the car just seemed to settle down and hug the road and we never even skidded.

We pulled up in front of Bert's place and Heath jumped out and ran up the walk, with me following him.

Amy Smith came to the door and I could see that she'd been crying, and she looked a little surprised to see the two of us.

We stood there for a moment without saying anything, then Heath spoke to her and here is a funny thing: Heath was wearing a pair of ragged overalls and a sweat-stained shirt and he didn't have a hat and his hair was all rumpled up, but there was a single instant when it seemed to me that he was well-dressed in an expensive business suit and that he took off his hat and bowed to Amy.

"I understand," he said, "that the little girl is sick. Maybe I can help."

I don't know if Amy had seen the same thing that I had seemed to see, but she opened the door and stood to one side so that we could enter.

"In there," she said.

"Thank you, ma'am," said Heath, and went into the room.

Amy and I stood there for a moment, then she turned to me and I could see the tears in her eyes again.

"Cal, she's awful sick," she said.

I nodded miserably, for now the spell was gone and common sense was coming back again and I wondered at the madness of this farmer who thought that he could help a little girl who was terribly sick. And at my madness for standing there, without even going in the room with him.

But just then Heath came out of the room and closed the door softly behind him.

"She's sleeping now," he said to Amy. "She'll be all right."

Then, without another word, he walked out of the door. I hesitated a moment, looking at Amy, wondering what to do. And it was pretty plain there was nothing I could do. So I followed him.

We drove back to his farm at a sober rate of speed, but the car banged and thumped just as bad as ever.

"Runs real good," I yelled at him.

He smiled a bit.

"I keep it tinkered up," he yelled back at me.

When we got to his place, I got out of his car and walked over to my own.

"You forgot the vegetables," he called after me.

So I went back to get them.

"Thanks a lot," I said.

"Anytime," he told me.

I looked straight at him, then, and said: "It sure would

be fine if we could get some rain. It would mean a lot to us. A soaking rain right now would save the corn."

"Come again," he told me. "It was good to talk with you."

And that night it rained, all over the valley, a steady, soaking rain, and the corn was saved.

And Ann got well.

The doctor, when he finally got to Bert's, said that she had passed the crisis and was already on the mend. One of those virus things, he said. A lot of it around. Not like the old days, he said, before they got to fooling around with all the miracle drugs, mutating viruses right and left. Used to be, he said, a doctor knew what he was treating, but he don't know anymore.

I don't know if Bert or Amy told Doc about Heath, although I imagine that they didn't. After all, you don't tell a doctor that a neighbor cured your child. And there might have been someone who would have been ornery enough to try to bring a charge against Heath for practicing medicine without a license, although that would have been pretty hard to prove. But the story got around the valley and there was a lot of talk. Heath, I heard, had been a famous doctor in Vienna before he'd made his getaway. But I didn't believe it. I don't even believe those who started the story believed it, but that's the way it goes in a neighborhood like ours.

That story, and others, made quite a flurry for a month or so, but then it quieted down and you could see that the Heaths had become one of us and belonged to the valley. Bert went over and had quite a talk with Heath and the womenfolks took to calling Mrs. Heath on the telephone, with some of those who were listening in breaking in to say a word or two, thereby initiating Mrs. Heath into the round-robin telephone conversations that are going on all the time on our valley party line, with it getting so that you have to bust in on them and tell them to get off the line when you want to make an important call. We had

Heath out with us on our coon hunts that fall and some of the young bloods started paying attention to Heath's daughter. It was almost as if the Heaths were old-time residents.

As I've said before, we've always been real fortunate in getting in good neighbors.

When things are going well, time has a way of flowing along so smoothly that you aren't conscious of its passing, and that was the way it was in the valley.

We had good years, but none of us paid much attention to that. You don't pay much attention to the good times, you get so you take them for granted. It's only when bad times come along that you look back and realize the good times you have had.

A year or so ago I was just finishing up the morning chores when a car with a New York license pulled up at the barnyard gate. It isn't very often we see an out-of-state license plate in the valley, so I figured that it probably was someone who had gotten lost and had stopped to ask directions. There was a man and woman in the front seat and three kids and a dog in the back seat and the car was new and shiny.

I was carrying the milk up from the barn and when the man got out I put the pails down on the ground and waited for him.

He was a youngish sort of fellow and he looked intelligent and he had good manners.

He told me his name was Rickard and that he was a New York newspaperman on vacation and had dropped into the valley on his way out west to check some information.

It was the first time, so far as I knew, that the valley had ever been of any interest newswise and I said so. I said we never did much here to get into the news.

"It's no scandal," Rickard told me, "if that is what you're thinking. It's just a matter of statistics."

There are a lot of times when I don't catch a situation

as quickly as I should, being a sort of deliberate type, but it seems to me now that as soon as he said statistics I could see it coming.

"I did a series of farm articles a few months back," said Rickard, "and to get my information I had to go through a lot of government statistics. I never got so sick of anything in my entire life."

"And?" I asked, not feeling too well myself.

"I found some interesting things about this valley," he went on. "I remember that I didn't catch it for a while. Went on past the figures for a ways. Almost missed the significance, in fact. Then I did a double take and backed up and looked at them again. The full story wasn't in that report, of course. Just a hint of something. So I did some more digging and came up with other facts."

I tried to laugh it off, but he wouldn't let me.

"Your weather, for one thing," he said. "Do you realize you've had perfect weather for the past ten years?"

"The weather's been pretty good," I admitted.

"It wasn't always good. I went back to see."

"That's right," I said. "It's been better lately."

"Your crops have been the best they've ever been in the last ten years."

"Better seed," I said. "Better ways of farming."

He grinned at me. "You guys haven't changed your way of farming in the last quarter-century."

And he had me there, of course.

"There was an army worm invasion two years ago," he said. "It hit all around you, but you got by scot-free."

"We were lucky. I remember we said so at the time."

"I checked the health records," he said. "Same thing once again. For ten solid years. No measles, no chicken pox, no pneumonia. No nothing. One death in ten full years—complications attendant on old age."

"Old Man Parks," I said. "He was going onto ninety. Fine old gentleman."

"You see," said Rickard.

I did see.

The fellow had the figures. He had tracked it down, this thing we hadn't even realized, and he had us cold.

"What do you want me to do about it?" I asked.

"I want to talk to you about a neighbor."

"I won't talk about any of my neighbors. Why don't you talk to him yourself?"

"I tried to, but he wasn't at home. Fellow down the road said he'd gone to town. Whole family had gone into town."

"Reginald Heath," I said. There wasn't much sense in playing dumb with Rickard, for he knew all the angles.

"That's the man. I talked to folks in town. Found out he'd never had to have any repair work done on any of his machinery or his car. Has the same machinery he had when he started farming. And it was worn out then."

"He takes good care of it," I told him. "He keeps it tinkered up."

"Another thing," said Rickard. "Since he's been here he hasn't bought a drop of gasoline."

I'd known the rest of it, of course, although I'd never stopped to think about it. But I didn't know about the gasoline. I must have shown my surprise, for Rickard grinned at me.

"What do you want?" I asked.

"A story."

"Heath's the man to talk to. I don't know a thing to help you."

And even when I said it I felt easy in my mind. I seemed to have an instinctive faith that Heath could handle the situation, that he'd know just what to do.

But after breakfast I couldn't settle down to work. I was pruning the orchard, a job I'd been putting off for a year or two and that badly needed doing. I kept thinking of that business of Heath not buying gasoline and that night I'd found the tractor plowing by itself and how smooth both the car and tractor ran despite all the noise they made.

So I laid down my pruning hook and shears and struck out across the fields. I knew the Heath family was in town, but I don't think it would have made any difference to me if they'd been at home. I think I would have gone just the same. For more than ten years now, I realized, I'd been wondering about that tractor and it was time that I found out.

I found the tractor in the machine shed and I thought maybe I'd have some trouble getting into it. But I didn't have a bit. I slipped the catches and the hood lifted up and I found exactly what I had thought I'd find, except that I hadn't actually worked out in my mind the picture of what I'd find underneath that hood.

It was just a block of some sort of shining metal that looked almost like a cube of heavy glass. It wasn't very big, but it had a massive look about it, as if it might have been a heavy thing to lift.

You could see the old bolt holes where the original internal combustion engine had been mounted and a heavy piece of some sort of metal had been fused across the frame to seat that little power plant. And up above the shiny cube was an apparatus of some sort. I didn't take the time to find out how it worked, but I could see that it was connected to the exhaust and knew it was a dingus that disguised the power plant. You know how in electric trains they have it fixed up so that the locomotive goes *chuff-chuff* and throws out a stream of smoke. Well, that was what that contraption was. It threw out little puffs of smoke and made a tractor noise.

I stood there looking at it and I wondered why it was, if Heath had an engine that worked better than an internal combustion engine, he should have gone to so much trouble to hide the fact he had it. If I'd had a thing like that, I knew I'd make the most of it. I'd get someone to back me and go into production and in no time at all I'd be stinking rich. And there'd be nothing in the world to prevent Heath from doing that. But instead he'd fixed the tractor so it looked and sounded like an ordinary tractor and he'd fixed his car to make so much noise that it hid the fact it had a new-type motor. Only he had overdone it. He'd made both the car and tractor make more noise than they should. And he'd missed an important bet in not buying gasoline. In his place I'd have bought the stuff, just the way you should, and thrown it away or burned it to get rid of it.

It almost seemed to me that Heath might have had something he was hiding all these years, that he'd tried deliberately to keep himself unnoticed. As if he might really have been a refugee from the Iron Curtain—or from somewhere else.

I put the hood back in place again and snapped the catches shut and when I went out I was very careful to shut the machine shed door securely.

I went back to my pruning and I did quite a bit of thinking and while I was doing it I realized that I'd been doing this same thinking, piecemeal, ever since that night I'd found the tractor running by itself. Thinking of it in snatches and not trying to correlate all my thinking and that way it hadn't added up to much, but now it did and I suppose I should have been a little scared.

But I wasn't scared. Reginald Heath was a neighbor, and a good one, and we'd gone hunting and fishing together and we'd helped one another with haying and threshing and one thing and another and I liked the man as well as anyone I had ever known. Sure, he was a little different and he had a funny kind of tractor and a funny kind of car and he might even have a way of stretching time and since he'd come into the valley we'd been fortunate in weather and in health. All true, of course, but nothing to be scared of. Nothing to be scared of, once you knew the man.

For some reason or other I remembered the time several years before when I'd dropped by of a summer evening. It was hot and the Heath family had brought chairs out on the lawn because it was cooler there. Heath got me a chair and we sat and talked, not about anything in particular, but whatever came into our heads.

There was no moon, but there were lots of stars and they were the prettiest I have ever seen them.

I called Heath's attention to them and, just shooting off my mouth, I told him what little I'd picked up about astronomy.

"They're a long ways off," I said. "So far off that their light takes years to reach us. And all of them are suns. A lot of them bigger than our sun."

Which was about all I knew about the stars.

Heath nodded gravely.

"There's one up there," he said, "that I watch a lot. That blue one, over there. Well, sort of blue, anyhow. See it? See how it twinkles. Like it might be winking at us. A friendly sort of star."

I pretended that I saw the one he was pointing at, although I wasn't sure I did, there were so many of them and a lot of them were twinkling.

Then we got to talking about something else and forgot about the stars. Or at least I did.

Right after supper, Bert Smith came over and said that Rickard had been around asking him some questions and that he'd been down to Jingo's place and that he'd said he'd see Heath just as soon as Heath got back from town.

Bert was a bit upset about it, so I tried to calm him down.

"These city folks get excited easy," I told him. "There's nothing to it."

I didn't worry much about it because I felt sure that Heath could handle things and even if Rickard did write a story for the New York papers it wouldn't bother us. Coon Valley is a long piece from New York.

I figured we'd probably seen and heard the last from

Rickard.

But in all my life, I've never been more wrong.

About midnight or so I woke up with Helen shaking me.

"There's someone at the door," she said. "Go see who it is."

So I shucked into my overalls and shoes and lit the lamp and went downstairs to see.

While I'd been getting dressed there'd been some knocking at the door, but as soon as I lit the lamp it quit.

I went to the door and opened it and there stood Rickard and he wasn't near as chipper as he'd been in the morning.

"Sorry to get you up," he said, "but it seems that I'm lost."

"You can't be lost," I told him. "There isn't but one road through the valley. One end of it ties up to Sixty and the other to Eighty-five. You follow the valley road and you're bound to hit one or the other of them."

"I've been driving," he told me, "for the last four hours and I can't find either of them."

"Look," I said, "all you do is drive one way or the other. You can't get off the road. Fifteen minutes either way and you're on the state highway."

I was exasperated with him, for it seemed a silly thing to do. And I don't take kindly to being routed out at midnight.

"But I tell you I'm lost," he said in a sort of desperation and I could see that he was close to panic. "The wife is getting scared and the kids are dead on their feet—"

"All right," I told him. "Let me get on my shirt and tie my shoes. I'll get you out of here."

He told me he wanted to get to Sixty, so I got out my car and told him to follow me. I was pretty sore about it, but I figured the only thing to do was to help him out. He'd upset the valley and the sooner out the better.

I drove for thirty minutes before I began to get

confused myself. That was twice as long as it should have taken to get out to the highway. But the road looked all right and there seemed to be nothing wrong, except for the time it took. So I kept on going. At the end of forty-five minutes we were back in front of my place again.

I couldn't figure it out for the life of me. I got out of my car and went back to Rickard's car.

"You see what I mean," he said.

"We must have got turned around," I said.

His wife was almost hysterical.

"What's going on?" she asked me in a high, shrill voice. "What is going on around here?"

"We'll try again," I said. "We'll drive slower this time so we don't make the same mistake."

I drove slower and this time it took an hour to get back to the farm. So we tried for Eighty-five and forty minutes later were right back where we started.

"I give up," I told them. "Get out and come in. We'll fix up some beds. You can spend the night and we'll get you out come light."

I cooked up some coffee and found stuff to make sandwiches while Helen fixed up beds to take care of the five of them.

"The dog can sleep out here in the kitchen," she said.

I got an apple box and quilt and fixed the dog a bed.

The dog was a nice little fellow, a wire-hair who was full of fun, and the Rickard kids were about as fine a bunch of kids as you'd find anywhere.

Mrs. Rickard was all set to have hysterics, but Helen got her to drink some coffee and I wouldn't let them talk about not being able to get out.

"Come daylight," I told them, "and there'll be nothing to it."

After breakfast they were considerably calmed down and seemed to have no doubt they could find Number Sixty. So they started out alone, but in an hour were back again. I took my car and started out ahead of them and I don't mind admitting I could feel bare feet walking up and down my spine.

I watched closely and all at once I realized that somehow we were headed back into the valley instead of heading out of it. So I stopped the car and we turned our cars around and headed back in the right direction. But in ten minutes we were turned around again. We tried again and this time we fairly crawled, trying to spot the place where we got turned around. But we could never spot it.

We went back to my place and I called up Bert and Jingo and asked them to come over.

Both of them tried to lead the Rickards out, one at a time, then the two of them together, but they were no better at it than I was. Then I tried it alone, without the Rickards following me, and I had no trouble at all. I was out to highway Sixty and back in half an hour. So we thought maybe the jinx was broken and I tried to lead out the Rickard car, but it was no soap.

By mid-afternoon we knew the answer. Any of the natives could get out of the valley, but the Rickards couldn't.

Helen put Mrs. Rickard to bed and fed her some sedative and I went over to see Heath.

He was glad to see me and he listened to me, but all the time I was talking to him I kept remembering how one time I had wondered if maybe he could stretch out time. When I had finished he was silent for a while, as if he might have been going over some decision just to be certain that it was right.

"It's a strange business, Calvin," he said finally, "and it doesn't seem right the Rickards should be trapped in this valley if they don't want to stay here.

"Yet, it's a fortunate thing for us, actually, Rickard was planning on writing a story about us, and if he'd written as he planned to, there'd been a lot of attention paid us. There would have been a crowd of people coming in—other newspapermen and government men and people from the universities and the idly curious. They'd have upset our lives and some of them would have offered us big sums of money for our farms, much more than they're worth, and all of it would spoil the valley for us. I don't know about you, but I like the valley as it is. It reminds me of. . . well, of another place."

"Rickard still can telephone that story," I told him, "or he can mail it out. Just keeping Rickard here won't prevent that story being printed."

"Somehow I think it will," he said. "I am fairly certain he won't telephone it or send it in the mails."

I had come half prepared to go to bat for Rickard, but I thought over what Heath had pointed out to me and I didn't do it.

I saw that if there were some principle or power which kept the valley healthy and insured good weather and made living pleasant, why, then, the rest of the world would be hell-bent to use the same principle or power. It might have been selfish of me, but I felt fairly certain the principle or power couldn't be spread thin enough to cover all the world. And if anyone were to have it, I wanted it kept right here, where it rightfully belonged.

And there was another thing: If the world should learn there was such a power or principle and if we couldn't share it or refused to share it, then all the world would be sore at us and we'd live in the center of a puddle of hatred.

I went back home and had a talk with Rickard and I didn't try to hide anything from him. He was all set to go and have it out with Heath, but I advised against it. I pointed out that he didn't have a shred of proof and he'd only make himself look silly, for Heath would more than likely act as if he didn't know what he was getting at. After quite a tussle, he took my advice.

The Rickards stayed on at our place for several days and occasionally Rickard and I would make a trial run just to test the situation out, but there was no change.

Finally Bert and Jingo came over and we had a council of war with the Rickard family. By this time Mrs. Rickard was taking it somewhat better and the Rickard kids were happy with the outdoor life and the Rickard dog was busily engaged in running all the valley rabbits down to skin and bones.

"There's the old Chandler place up at the head of the valley," said Jingo. "No one's been living there for quite a while, but it's in good shape. It could be fixed up so it was comfortable."

"But I can't stay here," protested Rickard. "I can't settle down here."

"Who said anything about settling down?" asked Bert. "You just got to wait it out. Some day whatever is wrong will get straightened out and then you can get away."

"But my job," said Rickard.

Mrs. Rickard spoke up then. You could see she didn't like the situation any better than he did, but she had the queer, practical, everyday logic that a woman at times surprised a man by showing. She knew that they were stuck here in the valley and she was out to make the best of it.

"Remember that book you're always threatening to write?" she asked. "Maybe this is it."

That did it.

Rickard mooned around for a while, making up his mind, although it already was made up. Then he began talking about the peace in the valley—the peace and quietness and the lack of hurry—just the place to write a book.

The neighbors got together and fixed up the house on the old Chandler place and Rickard called his office and made some excuse and got a leave of absence and wrote a letter to his bank, transferring whatever funds he had. Then he settled down to write.

Apparently in his phone calls and his letter writing he never even hinted at the real reason for his staying—

perhaps because it would have sounded downright silly—for there was no ruckus over his failure to go back.

The valley settled down to its normal life again and it felt good after all the uproar. The neighbors shopped for the Rickards and carried out from town all the groceries and other things they needed and once in a while Rickard took the car and had a try at finding the state highways.

But mostly he wrote and in about a year he sold this book of his. Probably you have read it: *You Could Hear the Silence*. Made him a hunk of money. But his New York publishers still are going slowly mad trying to understand why he steadfastly refuses to stir out of the valley. He has refused lecture tours, has declined dinners in his honor and turned down all the other glitter that goes with writing a best-seller.

The book didn't change Rickard at all. By the time he sold it he was well liked in the valley and seemed to like everyone—except possibly Heath. He stayed rather cold to Heath. He used to do a lot of walking, to get exercise, he said, although I think that he thought up most of his book out on those walks. And he'd stop by and chew the fat when he was out on those walks and that way everyone got to know him. He used to talk a lot about when he could get out of the valley and all of us were beginning to feel sorry that a time would come when he would leave, for the Rickards had turned out to be good neighbors. There must be something about the valley that brings out the best there is in everyone. As I have said before, we have yet to get a bad neighbor and that is something most neighborhoods can't say.

One day I had stopped on my way from town to talk a while with Heath and as we stood talking, up the road came Rickard. You could see he wasn't going anywhere, but was just out for a walk.

He stopped and talked with us for a few minutes, then suddenly he said, "You know, we've made up our minds that we would like to stay here."

"Now, that is fine," said Heath.

"Grace and I were talking about it the other night," said Rickard. "About the time when we could get out of here. Then suddenly we stopped our talking and looked at one another and we knew right then and there we didn't want to leave. It's been so peaceful and the kids like the school here so much better than in the city and the people are so fine we couldn't bear to leave."

"I'm glad to hear you say that," Heath told him. "But it seems to me you've been sticking pretty close. You ought to take the wife and kids in town to see a show."

And that was it. It was as simple as all that.

Life goes on in the valley as it always has, except it's even better now. All of us are healthy. We don't even seem to get colds any more. When we need rain we get it and when there's need for sun the sun is sure to shine. We aren't getting rich, for you can't get rich with all this Washington interference, but we're making a right good living. Rickard is working on his second book and once in a while I go out at night and try to locate the star Heath showed me that evening long ago.

But we still get some publicity now and then. The other night I was listening to my favorite newscaster and he had an item he had a lot of fun with.

"Is there really such a place as Coon Valley?" he asked and you could hear the chuckle just behind the words. "If there is, the government would like to know about it. The maps insist there is and there are statistics on the books that say it's a place where there is no sickness, where the climate is ideal, where there's never a crop failure—a land of milk and honey. Investigators have gone out to seek the truth of this and they can't find the place, although people in nearby communities insist there's such a valley. Telephone calls have been made to people listed as residents of the valley, but the calls can't be completed. Letters have been written to them, but the letters are returned to the sender for one or another of the many reasons the post office has for non-delivery. Investigators have waited in nearby trading centers, but Coon Valley people never came to town while the investigators were there. If there is such a place and if the things the statistics say of it are true, the government would be very interested, for there must be data in the valley that could be studied and applied to other sectors. We have no way of knowing whether this broadcast can reach the valley—if it is any more efficient than investigators or telephone or the post service. But if it does—and if there is such a place as Coon Valley—and if one of its residents should be listening, won't he please speak up!"

He chuckled then, chuckled very briefly, and went on to tell the latest rumor about Khrushchev.

I shut off the radio and sat in my chair and thought about the times when for several days no one could find his way out of the valley and of the other times when the telephones went dead for no apparent reason. And I remembered how we'd talked about it among ourselves and wondered if we should speak to Heath about it, but had in each case decided not to, since we felt that Heath knew what he was doing and that we could trust his judgment.

It's inconvenient at times, of course, but there are a lot of compensations. There hasn't been a magazine solicitor in the valley for more than a dozen years—nor an insurance salesman, either.

Over the River and Through the Woods

The two children came trudging down the lane in apple-canning time, when the first goldenrods were blooming and the wild asters large in bud. They looked, when she first saw them, out the kitchen window, like children who were coming home from school, for each of them was carrying a bag in which might have been their books. Like Charles and James, she thought, like Alice and Maggie—but the time when those four had trudged the lane on their daily trips to school was in the distant past. Now they had children of their own who made their way to school.

She turned back to the stove to stir the cooking apples, for which the wide-mouthed jars stood waiting on the table, then once more looked out the kitchen window. The two of them were closer now and she could see that the boy was the older of the two—ten, perhaps, and the girl no more than eight.

They might be going past, she thought, although that did not seem too likely, for the lane led to this farm and to nowhere else.

They turned off the lane before they reached the barn and came sturdily trudging up the path that led to the house. There was no hesitation in them; they knew where they were going.

She stepped to the screen door of the kitchen as they came onto the porch and they stopped before the door and stood looking up at her.

The boy said, "You are our grandma. Papa said we were to say at once that you were our grandma."

"But that's not. . .," she said, and stopped. She had been about to say that it was impossible that she was their grandma. And, looking down into the sober, childish faces, she was glad that she had not said the words.

"I am Ellen," said the girl, in a piping voice.

"Why, that is strange," the woman said. "That is my name, too."

The boy said, "My name is Paul."

She pushed open the door for them and they came in, standing silently in the kitchen, looking all about them as if they'd never seen a kitchen.

"It's just like Papa said," said Ellen. "There's the stove and the churn and. . ."

The boy interrupted her. "Our name is Forbes," he said.

This time the woman couldn't stop herself. "Why, that's impossible," she said. "That is our name, too."

The boy nodded solemnly. "Yes, we knew it was."

"Perhaps," the woman said, "you'd like some milk and cookies."

"Cookies!" Ellen squealed, delighted.

"We don't want to be any trouble," said the boy. "Papa said we were to be no trouble."

"He said we should be good," piped Ellen.

"I am sure you will be," said the woman, "and you are no trouble."

In a little while, she thought, she'd get it straightened out.

She went to the stove and set the kettle with the cooking apples to one side, where they would simmer slowly.

"Sit down at the table," she said. "I'll get the milk and cookies."

She glanced at the clock, ticking on the shelf. Four o'clock, almost. In just a little while the men would come in from the fields. Jackson Forbes would know what to do about this; he had always known.

They climbed up on two chairs and sat there solemnly, staring all about them, at the ticking clock, at the woodstove with the fire glow showing through its draft, at the wood piled in the wood box, at the butter churn standing in the corner.

They set their bags on the floor beside them, and they were strange bags, she noticed. They were made of heavy cloth or canvas, but there were no drawstrings or no straps to fasten them. But they were closed, she saw, despite no straps or strings.

"Do you have some stamps?" asked Ellen.

"Stamps?" asked Mrs. Forbes.

"You must pay no attention to her," said Paul. "She should not have asked you. She asks everyone and Mama told her not to."

"But stamps?"

"She collects them. She goes around snitching letters that other people have. For the stamps on them, you know."

"Well now," said Mrs. Forbes, "there may be some old letters. We'll look for them later on."

She went into the pantry and got the earthen jug of milk and filled a plate with cookies from the jar. When she came back they were sitting there sedately, waiting for the cookies.

"We are here just for a little while," said Paul. "Just a short vacation. Then our folks will come and get us and take us back again."

Ellen nodded her head vigorously. "That's what they told us when we went. When I was afraid to go."

"You were afraid to go?"

"Yes. It was all so strange."

"There was so little time," said Paul. "Almost none at all. We had to leave so fast."

"And where are you from?" asked Mrs. Forbes.

"Why," said the boy, "just a little ways from here. We walked just a little ways and of course we had the map. Papa gave it to us and he went over it carefully with us. . ."

"You're sure your name is Forbes?"

Ellen bobbed her head. "Of course it is," she said.

"Strange," said Mrs. Forbes. And it was more than strange, for there were no other Forbes in the neighborhood except her children and her grandchildren and these two, no matter what they said, were strangers.

They were busy with the milk and cookies and she went back to the stove and set the kettle with the apples back on the front again, stirring the cooking fruit with a wooden spoon.

"Where is Grandpa?" Ellen asked.

"Grandpa's in the field. He'll be coming in soon. Are you finished with your cookies?"

"All finished," said the girl.

"Then we'll have to set the table and get the supper cooking. Perhaps you'd like to help me."

Ellen hopped down off the chair. "I'll help," she said.

"And I," said Paul, "will carry in some wood. Papa said I should be helpful. He said I could carry in the wood and feed the chickens and hunt the eggs and. . ."

"Paul," said Mrs. Forbes, "it might help if you'd tell me what your father does."

"Papa," said the boy, "is a temporal engineer."

The two hired men sat at the kitchen table with the checker board between them. The two older people were in the living room.

"You never saw the likes of it," said Mrs. Forbes. "There was this piece of metal and you pulled it and it ran along another metal strip and the bag came open. And you pulled it the other way and the bag was closed."

"Something new," said Jackson Forbes. "There may be many new things we haven't heard about, back here in the sticks. There are inventors turning out all sorts of things."

"And the boy," she said, "has the same thing on his trousers. I picked them up from where he threw them on the floor when he went to bed and I folded them and put them on the chair. And I saw this strip of metal, the edges jagged-like. And the clothes they wear. That boy's trousers are cut off above the knees and the dress that the girl was wearing was so short. . ."

"They talked of plains," mused Jackson Forbes, "but not the plains we knew. Something that is used, apparently, for folks to travel in. And rockets—as if there were rockets every day and not just on the Earth."

"We couldn't question them, of course," said Mrs. Forbes. "There was something about them, something that I sensed."

Her husband nodded. "They were frightened, too."

"You are frightened, Jackson?"

"I don't know," he said, "but there are no other Forbes. Not close, that is. Charlie is the closest and he's five miles away. And they said they walked just a little piece."

"What are you going to do?" she asked. "What can we do?"

"I don't rightly know," he said. "Drive in to the county seat and talk with the sheriff, maybe. These children must be lost. There must be someone looking for them."

"But they don't act as if they're lost," she told him. "They knew they were coming here. They knew we would be here. They told me I was their grandma and they asked after you and they called you Grandpa. And they are so sure. They don't act as if we're strangers. They've been told about us. They said they'd stay just a little while and that's the way they act. As if they'd just come for a visit."

"I think," said Jackson Forbes, "that I'll hitch up Nellie

after breakfast and drive around the neighborhood and ask some questions. Maybe there'll be someone who can tell me something."

"The boy said his father was a temporal engineer. That just don't make sense. Temporal means the worldly power and authority and. . ."

"It might be some joke," her husband said. "Something that the father said in jest and the son picked up as truth."

"I think," said Mrs. Forbes, "I'll go upstairs and see if they're asleep. I left their lamps turned low. They are so little and the house is strange to them. If they are asleep, I'll blow out the lamps."

Jackson Forbes grunted his approval. "Dangerous," he said, "to keep lights burning of the night. Too much chance of fire."

The boy was asleep, flat upon his back—the deep and healthy sleep of youngsters. He had thrown his clothes upon the floor when he had undressed to go to bed, but now they were folded neatly on the chair, where she had placed them when she had gone into the room to say goodnight.

The bag stood beside the chair and it was open, the two rows of jagged metal gleaming dully in the dim glow of the lamp. Within its shadowed interior lay the dark forms of jumbled possesions, disorderly, and helter-skelter, no way for a bag to be.

She stooped and picked up the bag and set it on the chair and reached for the little metal tab to close it. At least, she told herself, it should be closed and not left standing open. She grasped the tab and it slid smoothly along the metal tracks and then stopped, its course obstructed by an object that stuck out.

She saw it was a book and reached down to rearrange it so she could close the bag. And as she did so, she saw the title in its faint gold lettering across the leather backstrap—Holy Bible.

With her fingers grasping the book, she hesitated for a moment, then slowly drew it out. It was bound in an expensive black leather that was dulled with age. The edges were cracked and split and the leather worn from long usage. The gold edging of the leaves was faded.

Hesitantly, she opened it and there, upon the flyleaf, in old and faded ink, was the inscription:

To Sister Ellen
from Amelia
Oct. 30, 1896
Many Happy Returns of the Day

She felt her knees grow weak and she let herself carefully to the floor and there, crouched beside the chair, read the flyleaf once again.

30 October 1896—that was her birthday, certainly, but it had not come as yet, for this was only the beginning of September, 1896.

And the Bible—how old was this Bible she held within her hands? A hundred years, perhaps, more than a hundred years.

A Bible, she thought—exactly the kind of gift Amelia would give her. But a gift that had not been given yet, one that could not be given, for that day upon the flyleaf was a month into the future.

It couldn't be, of course. It was some kind of stupid joke. Or some mistake. Or a coincidence, perhaps. Somewhere else someone else was named Ellen and also had a sister who was named Amelia and the date was a mistake—someone had written the wrong year. It would be an easy thing to do.

But she was not convinced. They had said the name was Forbes and they had come straight here and Paul had spoken of a map so they could find the way.

Perhaps there were other things inside the bag. She looked at it and shook her head. She shouldn't pry. It had been wrong to take the Bible out.

On 30 October she would be fifty-nine—an old farm-wife with married sons and daughters and grandchildren who came to visit her on weekends and on holidays. And a sister Amelia who, in this year of 1896, would give her a Bible as a birthday gift.

Her hands shook as she lifted the Bible and put it back into the bag. She'd talk to Jackson when she went downstairs. He might have some thought upon the matter and he'd know what to do.

She tucked the book back into the bag and pulled the tab and the bag was closed. She set it on the floor again and looked at the boy upon the bed. He still was fast asleep, so she blew out the light.

In the adjoining room little Ellen slept, baby-like, upon her stomach. The low flame of the turned-down lamp flickered gustily in the breeze that came through an open window.

Ellen's bag was closed and stood squared against the chair with a sense of neatness. The woman looked at it and hesitated for a moment, then moved on around the bed to where the lamp stood on a bedside table.

The children were asleep and everything was well and she'd blow out the light and go downstairs and talk with Jackson, and perhaps there'd be no need for him to hitch up Nellie in the morning and drive around to ask questions of the neighbors.

As she leaned to blow out the lamp, she saw the envelope upon the table, with the two large stamps of many colors affixed to the upper right-hand corner.

Such pretty stamps, she thought—I never saw so pretty. She leaned closer to take a look at them and saw the country name upon them. Israel. But there was no such actual place as Israel. It was a Bible name, but there was no country. And if there were no country, how could there be stamps?

She picked up the envelope and studied the stamp, making sure that she had seen right. Such a pretty stamp!

She collects them, Paul had said. She's always snitching letters that belong to other people.

The envelope bore a postmark, and presumably a date, but it was blurred and distorted by a hasty, sloppy cancellation and she could not make it out.

The edge of a letter sheet stuck a quarter inch out of the ragged edges where the envelope had been torn open and she pulled it out, gasping in her haste to see it while an icy fist of fear was clutching at her heart.

It was, she saw, only the end of a letter, the last page of a letter, and it was in type rather than in longhand—type like one saw in a newspaper or a book.

Maybe one of those new-fangled things they had in big city offices, she thought, the ones she'd read about. Typewriters—was that what they were called?

do not believe, the one page read, *your plan is feasible. There is no time. The aliens are closing in and they will not give us time.*

And there is the further consideration of the ethics of it, even if it could be done. We cannot, in all conscience, scurry back into the past and visit our problems upon the people of a century ago. Think of the problems it would create for them, the economic confusion and the psychological effect.

If you feel that you must, at least, send the children back, think a moment of the wrench it will give those two good souls when they realize the truth. Theirs is a snug and solid world—sure and safe and sound. The concepts of this mad century would destroy all they have, all that they believe in.

But I suppose I cannot presume to counsel you. I have done what you asked. I have written you all I know of our old ancestors back on that Wisconsin farm. As historian of the family, I am sure my facts are right. Use them as you see fit and God have mercy on us all.

Your loving brother,
Jackson

P.S. A suggestion. If you do send the children back, you might send along with them a generous supply of the new cancer-inhibitor drug. Great-great-grandmother Forbes died in 1904 of a condition that I suspect was cancer. Given those pills, she might survive another ten or twenty years. And what, I ask you brother, would that mean to this tangled future? I don't pretend to know. It might save us. It might kill us quicker. It might have no effect at all. I leave the puzzle to you.

If I can finish up work here and get away, I'll be with you at the end.

Mechanically she slid the letter back into the envelope and laid it upon the table beside the flaring lamp.

Slowly she moved to the window that looked out out on the empty lane.

They will come and get us, Paul had said. But would they ever come. Could they ever come?

She found herself wishing they would come. Those poor people, those poor frightened children caught so far in time.

Blood of my blood, she thought, flesh of my flesh, so many years away. But still her flesh and blood, no matter how removed. Not only these two beneath this roof tonight, but all those others who had not come to her.

The letter had said 1904 and cancer and that was eight years away—she'd be an old, old woman then. And the signature had been Jackson—an old family name, she wondered, carried on and on, a long chain of people who bore the name of Jackson Forbes?

She was stiff and numb, she knew. Later she'd be frightened. Later she would wish she had not read the letter. Perhaps, she did not know.

But now she must go back downstairs and tell Jackson the best way that she could.

She moved across the room and blew out the light and went out into the hallway.

A voice came from the open door beyond.

"Grandma, is that you?"

"Yes, Paul," she answered. "What can I do for you?"

In the doorway she saw him crouched beside the chair, in the shaft of moonlight pouring through the window, fumbling at the bag.

"I forgot," he said. "There was something Papa said I was to give you right away."

Construction Shack

In that same year when men first walked on Mars the probe was launched from the moon for Pluto. Five years later the first pictures were transmitted as the orbiting probe trained its cameras on the planet's surface. The transmission quality was poor; but even so, certain features of the photographs were productive of great anguish as old theories fell to shards and were replaced by puzzlement, questions with no hint of answers. The pictures seemed to say that the planet had a smooth, almost polished surface, without a single geographic feature to break the smoothness of it. Except that at certain places, equidistant from one another along the equator, were tiny dots that would have been taken for transmission noise if they had not appeared consistently. Too, the dots still persisted when some of the noise was eliminated. So it seemed they must be small geographic features or shadows cast by geographic features, although at Pluto's distance from the sun shadows would be suspect. The other data did nothing to lessen the anguish. The planet was smaller than supposed, less than a thousand miles in diameter, and its density worked out to 3.5 grams per cubic centimeter rather than the unrealistic figure of 60 grams, previously supposed.

This meant several things. It meant that somewhere out there, perhaps something more than seven billion miles from the sun, a tenth planet of the solar system swung in orbit, for no planet the size and mass of Pluto could explain the eccentricities in the orbits of Uranus and Neptune. The calculation of Pluto's mass, now proved inaccurate, had been based on the measurement of those eccentricities and it must be admitted now that something else must account for them.

Beyond that, Pluto was most strange—a smooth planet, featureless except for the evenly spaced dots. The smoothness certainly could not be explained by a non-turbulent atmosphere, for surely Pluto had to be too small and cold to hold an atmosphere. A surface of ice, men wondered, the frozen remnants of a one-time, momentary atmosphere? But for a number of reasons that didn't seem right, either. Metal, perhaps, but if the planet were of solid metal the density should be far greater.

The men on Earth consoled themselves. In five more years the probe would come back to Earth, carrying with it the films that it had taken and from them, the actual films and not the low-quality transmissions, perhaps much that was hazy now might become understandable. The probe swung in its measured orbits and sent back more pictures, although they were little help, for the quality still was poor. Then it fired the automatic sequence that would head it back to Earth, and its beeping signals from far out in space said it was headed home on a true and steady course.

Something happened. The beeping stopped and there was a silence. Moon Base waited. It might start up again. The silence might indicate only a momentary malfunction and the signals might start again. But they never did. Somewhere, some three billion miles from the sun, some mishap had befallen the homing probe. It was never heard again—it was lost forever.

There was no sense in sending out another probe until a day when technical advances could assure better pictures. The technical advances would have to be significant—small refinements would do little good.

The second and third manned expeditions went to Mars and came back home again, bringing back, among many other things, evidence that primitive forms of life existed here, which settled once and for all the old, dark suspicion that life might be an aberration to be found only on the Earth. For with life on two planets in the same solar system there could no longer be any doubt that life was a common factor in the universe. The fourth expedition went out, landed and did not come back again and now there was on Mars a piece of ground that was forever Earth. The fifth expedition was sent out even while the Earth still paid tribute to those four men who had died so far from home.

Now that life had been found on another world, now that it was apparent that another planet at one time had held seas and rivers and an atmosphere that had been an approximation of Earth's own atmosphere, now that we knew we no longer were alone in the universe, the public interest and support of space travel revived. Scientists, remembering (never having, in fact, forgotten, for it had gnawed steadily at their minds) the puzzlement of the Pluto probe, began to plan a manned Pluto expedition, as there was still no sense in sending an instrumented probe.

When the day came to lift from the Moon Base, I was a member of the expedition. I went along as a geologist—the last thing a Pluto expedition needed.

There were three of us and any psychologist will tell you that three is a number that is most unfortunate. Two gang up on one or ignore one and there is always competition to be one of the gang of two. No one wants to stand alone with the other two against him. But it didn't work that way with us. We got along all right, although there were times when it was rough going. The five years that the probe took to arrive at Pluto was cut by more than half, not only because of improved rocket capability, but because a manned craft could pile on velocity that couldn't be programmed—or at least safely programmed—into a probe. But a bit more than two years is a long time to be cooped up in a tin can rocketing along in emptiness. Maybe it wouldn't be so bad if you had some sense of speed, of really getting somewhere—but you haven't. You just hang there in space.

The three of us? Well, I am Howard Lunt and the other two men were Orson Gates, a chemist, and Tyler Hampton, an engineer.

As I say, we got along fine. We played chess tournaments—yeah, three men in a tournament and it was all right because none of us knew chess. If we had been any good I suppose we would have been at one another's throats. We dreamed up dirty ditties and were so pleased with our accomplishments that we'd spend hours singing them and none of us could sing. We did a lot of other futile things—by now you should be getting the idea. There were some rather serious scientific experiments and observations we were supposed to make, but all of us figured that our first and biggest job was to manage to stay sane.

When we neared Pluto we dropped the fooling around and spent much time peering through the scope, arguing and speculating about what we saw. Not that there was much to see. The planet resembled nothing quite as much as a billiard ball. It was smooth. There were no mountains, no valleys, no craters—nothing marred the smoothness of the surface. The dots were there, of course. We could make out seven groups of them, all positioned along the equatorial belt. And in close-up they were not simply dots. They were structures of some kind.

We landed finally, near a group of them. The landing was a little harder than we had figured it would be. The planetary surface was hard—there was no give to it. But we stayed right-side up and we didn't break a thing.

People at times ask me to describe Pluto and it's a hard thing to put into words. You can say that it is smooth and that it's dark—it's dark even in broad daylight. The sun, at that distance, is not much more than a slightly brighter star. You don't have daylight on Pluto—you have starlight and it doesn't make much difference whether you're facing the sun or not. The planet is airless, of course, and waterless and cold. But cold, as far as human sensation is concerned, is a relative thing. Once the temperature gets down to a hundred Kelvin it doesn't much matter how much colder it becomes. Especially when you're wearing life support. Without a suit containing life support, you'd last only a few seconds, if that long, on a place like Pluto. I've never figured out which would kill you first—cold or internal pressure. Would you freeze, or explode before you froze?

So Pluto is dark, airless, cold and smooth. Those are the externals only. You stand there and look at the sun and realize how far away you are. You know you are standing at the edge of the solar system, that just out there, a little way beyond, you'd be clear outside the system. Which doesn't really have to be true, of course. You know about the tenth planet. Even if it's theory, it's supposed to be out there. You know about the millions of circling comets that technically are a part of the solar system, although they're so far out no one ever thinks of them. You could say to yourself this really is not the edge—the hypothetical tenth planet and the comets are still out there. But this is intellectualization; you're telling yourself something that your mind says may be true, but your gut denies. For hundreds of years Pluto has been the last outpost and this, by God, is Pluto and you're farther away from home than man has ever been before and you feel it. You don't belong to anything any more. You're in the back alley, and the bright and happy streets are so far away that you know you'll never find them.

It isn't homesickness that you feel. It's more like never having had a home. Of never having belonged anywhere. You get over it, of course—or come to live with it.

So we came down out of the ship after we had landed and stood upon the surface. The first thing that struck us—other than the sense of lostness that at once grabbed all of us—was that the horizon was too near, much nearer than on the Moon. We felt at once that we stood on a small world. We noticed that horizon's nearness even before we noticed the buildings that the probe had photographed as dots and that we had dropped down to investigate. Perhaps buildings is not the right word—structures probably would be better. Buildings are enclosures and these were not enclosures. They were domes someone had set out to build and hadn't had time to finish. The basic underlying framework had been erected and then the work had stopped. Riblike arcs curved up from the surface and met overhead. Struts and braces held the frames solid, but that was as far as the construction had gone. There were three of them, one larger than the other two. The frames were not quite as simple as I may have made them seem. Tied into the ribs and struts and braces were a number of other structural units that seemed to have no purpose and make no sense at all.

We tried to make sense out of them and out of the scooped-out hollows that had been gouged out of the planetary surface within the confines of each construct—they had no floors and seemed fastened to the surface of the planet. The hollows were circular, some six feet across and three feet deep, and to me they looked like nothing quite as much as indentations made in a container of ice cream by a scoop.

About this time Tyler began to have some thoughts about the surface. Tyler is an engineer and should have had his thoughts immediately—and so should the rest of us—but the first hour or so outside the ship had been considerably confusing. We had worn our suits in training, of course, and had done some walking around in them, but Pluto seemed to have even less gravity than had been calculated and we had to get used to it before we could be reasonably comfortable. Nor had anything else been exactly as we had anticipated.

"This surface," Tyler said to me. "There is something wrong with it."

"We knew it was smooth," said Orson. "The pictures showed that. Coming in, we could see it for ourselves."

"This smooth?" Tyler asked. "This even?" He turned to me. "It isn't geologically possible. Would you say it is?"

"I would think not," I said. "If there had been any upheaval at all this floor would be rugged. There can't have been any erosion—anything to level it down. Micrometeorite impacts, maybe, but not too many of them. We're too far out for meteorites of any size. And while micrometeorites might pit the surface there would be no levelling process."

Tyler let himself down on his knees rather awkwardly. He brushed a hand across the surface. The seeing was not too good, but you could see that there was dust, a thin layer of dust, a powdering.

"Shine a light down here," said Tyler.

Orson aimed his light at the spot. Some of the grey dust still clung where Tyler had wiped his hand, but there were streaks where the darker surface showed through.

"Space dust," said Tyler.

Orson said, "There should be damn little of it."

"True," said Tyler. "But over four billion years or

more, it would accumulate. It couldn't be erosion dust, could it?"

"Nothing to cause erosion," I said. "This must be as close to a dead planet as you ever get. Not enough gravity to hold any of the gases—if there ever were gases. At one time there must have been, but they've all gone—they went early. No atmosphere, no water. I doubt there ever was any accumulation. A molecule wouldn't hang around for long."

"But space dust would?"

"Maybe. Some sort of electrostatic attraction, maybe."

Tyler scrubbed the little patch of surface again with his gloved hand, removing more of the dust, with more of the darker surface showing through.

"Have we got a drill?" he asked. "A specimen drill."

"I have one in my kit," said Orson. He took it out and handed it to Tyler. Tyler positioned the bit against the surface, pressed the button. In the light of the torch you could see the bit spinning. Tyler put more weight on the drill.

"It's harder than a bitch," he said.

The bit began to bite. A small pile of fragments built up around the hole. The surface was hard, no doubt of that. The bit didn't go too deep and the pile of fragments was small.

Tyler gave up. He lifted out the bit and snubbed off the motor.

"Enough for analysis?" he asked.

"Should be," said Orson. He took the bit from Tyler and handed him a small specimen bag. Tyler laid the open mouth of the bag on the surface and brushed the fragments into it.

"Now we'll know," he said. "Now we will know something."

A couple of hours later, back in the ship, we knew.

"I have it," Orson said, "but I don't believe it."

"Metal?" asked Tyler.

"Sure, metal. But not the kind you have in mind. It's steel."

"Steel?" I said, horrified. "It can't be. Steel's no natural metal. It's manufactured."

"Iron," said Orson. "Nickel. Molybdenum, vanadium, chromium. That works out to steel. I don't know as much about steel as I should. But it's steel—a good steel. Corrosion resistant, tough, strong."

"Maybe just the platform for the structures," I said. "Maybe a pad of steel to support them. We took the specimen close to one of them."

"Let's find out," said Tyler.

We opened up the garage and ran down the ramp and got out the buggy. Before we left we turned off the television camera. By this time Moon Base would have seen all they needed to see and if they wanted more they could ask for it. We had given them a report on everything we had found—all except the steel surface and the three of us agreed that until we knew more about that we would not say anything. It would be a while in any case until we got an answer from them. The time lag to Earth was about sixty hours each way.

We went out ten miles and took a boring sample and came back, following the thin tracks the buggy made in the dust, taking samples every mile. We got the answer that I think all of us expected we would get, but couldn't bring ourselves to talk about. The samples were all steel.

It didn't seem possible, of course, and it took us a while to digest the fact, but finally we admitted that on the basis of best evidence Pluto was no planet, but a fabricated metal ball, small-planet size. But God-awful big for anyone to build.

Anyone?

That was the question that now haunted us. Who had built it? Perhaps more important—why had they built it? For some purpose, surely, but why, once that purpose had been fulfilled (if, in fact, it had been fulfilled) had

Pluto been left out here at the solar system's rim?

"No one from the system," Tyler said. "There's no one but us. Mars has life, of course, but primitive life. It got a start there and hung on and that was all. Venus is too hot. Mercury is too close to the sun. The big gas planets? Maybe, but not the kind of life that would build a thing like this. It had to be something from outside."

"How about the fifth planet?" suggested Orson.

"There probably never was a fifth planet," I said. "The material for it may have been there, but the planet never formed. By all the rules of celestial mechanics there should have been a planet between Mars and Jupiter, but something went haywire."

"The tenth planet, then," said Orson.

"No one is really positive there is a tenth," said Tyler.

"Yeah, you're right," said Orson. "Even if there were, it would be a poor bet for life, let alone intelligence."

"So that leaves us with outsiders," said Tyler.

"And a long time ago," said Orson.

"Why do you say that?"

"The dust. There isn't much dust in the universe."

"And no one knows what it is. There is the dirty ice theory."

"I see what you're getting at. But it needn't be ice. Nor graphite, nor any of the other things that have been—"

"You mean it's that stuff out there."

"It could be. What do you think, Howard?"

"I can't be sure," I said. "The only thing I know is that it couldn't be erosive."

Before we went to sleep we tried to fix up a report to beam back to Moon Base, but anything we put together sounded too silly and unbelievable. So we gave up. We'd have to tell them some time, but we could wait.

When we awoke we had a bite to eat, then got into our suits and went out to look over the structures. They still didn't make much sense, especially all the crazy contraptions that were fastened on the ribs and struts and braces. Nor did the scooped-out hollows.

"If they were only up on legs," said Orson, "they could be used as chairs."

"But not very comfortable," said Tyler.

"If you tilted them a bit," said Orson. But that didn't figure either. They would still be uncomfortable. I wondered why he thought of them as chairs. They didn't look like any chairs to me.

We pottered around a lot, not getting anywhere. We looked the structures over inch by inch, wondering all the while if there was something we had missed. But there didn't seem to be.

Now comes the funny part of it. I don't know why we did it—out of sheer desperation, maybe. But failing to find any clues, we got down on our hands and knees, dusting at the surface with our hands. What we hoped to find, I don't know. It was slow going and it was a dirty business, with the dust tending to stick to us.

"If we'd only brought some brooms along," said Orson.

But we had no brooms. Who in his right mind would have thought we would want to sweep a planet?

So there we were. We had what appeared to be a manufactured planet and we had some stupid structures for which we could deduce not a single reason. We had come a long way and we had been expected to make some tremendous discovery once we landed. We had made a discovery, all right, but it didn't mean a thing.

We finally gave up with the sweeping business and stood there, scuffing our feet and wondering what to do next when Tyler suddenly let out a yell and pointed at a place on the surface where his boots had kicked away the dust.

We all bent to look at what he had found. We saw three holes in the surface, each an inch or so across and some three inches deep, placed in a triangle and close together. Tyler got down on his hands and knees and shone his light down into the holes, each one of them in turn.

Finally he stood up. "I don't know," he said. "They could maybe be a lock of some sort. Like a combination. There are little notches on the sides, down at the bottom of them. If you moved those notches just right something might happen."

"Might blow ourselves up, maybe," said Orson. "Do it wrong and bang!"

"I don't think so," said Tyler. "I don't think it's anything like that. I don't say it's a lock, either. But I don't think it's a bomb. Why should they booby-trap a thing like this?"

"You can't tell what they might have done," I said. "We don't know what kind of things they were or why they were here."

Tyler didn't answer. He got down again and began carefully dusting the surface, shining his light on it while he dusted. We didn't have anything else to do, so we helped him.

It was Orson who found it this time—a hairline crack you had to hold your face down close to the surface to see. Having found it, we did some more dusting and worried it out. The hairline described a circle and the three holes were set inside and to one edge of it. The circle was three feet or so in diameter.

"Either of you guys good at picking locks?" said Tyler.

Neither of us were.

"It's got to be a hatch of some sort," Orson said. "This metal ball we're standing on has to be a hollow ball. If it weren't its mass would be greater than it is."

"And no one," I said, "would be insane enough to build a solid ball. It would take too much metal and too much energy to move."

"You're sure that it was moved?" asked Orson.

"It had to be," I told him. "It wasn't built in this system. No one here could have built it."

Tyler had pulled a screwdriver out of his tool kit and was poking into the hole with it.

"Wait a minute," said Orson. "I just thought of something."

He nudged Tyler to one side, reached down and inserted three fingers into the holes and pulled. The circular section rose smoothly on its hinges.

Wedged into the area beneath the door were objects that looked like the rolls of paper you buy to wrap up Christmas presents. Bigger than rolls of paper, though. Six inches or so across.

I got hold of one of them and that first one was not easy to grip, for they were packed in tightly. But I managed with much puffing and grunting to pull it out. It was heavy and a good four feet in length.

Once we got one out, the other rolls were easier to lift. We pulled out three more and headed for the ship.

But before we left I held the remaining rolls over to one side, to keep them from tilting, while Orson shone his light down into the hole. We had half expected to find a screen or something under the rolls, with the hole extending on down into a cavity that might have been used as living quarters or a workroom. But the hole ended in machined metal. We could see the grooves left by the drill or die that had bored the hole. That hole had just one purpose, to store the rolls we had found inside it.

Back in the ship we had to wait a while for the rolls to pick up some heat before we could handle them. Even so we had to wear gloves when we began to unroll them. Now, seeing them in good light, we realized that they were made up of many sheets rolled up together. The sheets seemed to be made of some sort of extremely thin metal or tough plastic. They were stiff from the cold and we spread them out on our lone table and weighted them down to hold them flat.

On the first sheet were diagrams of some sort,

drawings and what might have been specifications written into the diagrams and along the margins. The specifications, of course, meant nothing to us (although later some were puzzled out and mathematicians and chemists were able to figure out some of the formulas and equations).

"Blueprints," said Tyler. "This whole business was an engineering job."

"If that's the case," said Orson, "those strange things fastened to the structural frames could be mounts to hold engineering instruments."

"Could be," said Tyler.

"Maybe the instruments are stored in some other holes like the one where we found the blueprints," I suggested.

"I don't think so," said Tyler. "They would have taken the instruments with them when they left."

"Why didn't they take the blueprints, too?"

"The instruments would have been worthwhile to take. They could be used on another job. But the blueprints couldn't. And there may have been many sets of prints and spec sheets. These we have may be only one of many sets of duplicates. There would have been a set of master prints and those they might have taken with them when they left."

"What I don't understand," I said, "is what they could have been building out here. What kind of construction? And why here? I suppose we could think of Pluto as a massive construction shack, but why exactly here? With all the galaxy to pick from, why this particular spot?"

"You ask too many questions all at once," Orson told me.

"Let's look," said Tyler. "Maybe we'll find out."

He peeled the first sheet off the top and let it drop to the floor. It snapped back to the rolled-up position.

The second sheet told us nothing, nor did the third or fourth. Then came the fifth sheet.

"Now, here is something," said Tyler.

We leaned closer to look.

"It's the solar system," Orson said.

I counted rapidly, "Nine planets."

"Where's the tenth?" asked Orson. "There should be a tenth."

"Something's wrong," said Tyler. "I don't know what it is."

I spotted it. "There's a planet between Mars and Jupiter."

"That means there is no Pluto shown," said Orson.

"Of course not," said Tyler. "Pluto never was a planet."

"Then this means there once actually was a planet between Mars and Jupiter," said Orson.

"Not necessarily," Tyler told him. "It may only mean there was supposed to be."

"What do you mean?"

"They bungled the job," said Tyler. "They did a sloppy piece of engineering."

"You're insane!" I shouted at him.

"Your blind spot is showing, Howard. According to what we think, perhaps it is insane. According to the theories our physicists have worked out. There is a cloud of dust and gas and the cloud contracts to form a protostar. Our scientists have invoked a pretty set of phyical laws to calculate what happens. Physical laws that were automatic—since no one would be mad enough to postulate a gang of cosmic engineers who went about the universe building solar systems."

"But the tenth planet," persisted Orson. "There has to be a tenth planet. A big, massive—"

"They messed up the projected fifth planet," Tyler said. "God knows what else they messed up. Venus, maybe. Venus shouldn't be the kind of planet it is. It should be another Earth, perhaps a slightly warmer Earth, but not the hell hole it is. And Mars. They loused that up, too. Life started there, but it never had a chance.

It hung on and that was all. And Jupiter. Jupiter is a monstrosity—"

"You think the only reason for a planet's existence is its capability of supporting life?"

"I don't know, of course. But it should be in the specs. Three planets that could have been life-bearing and of these only one was successful."

"Then," said Orson, "there could be a tenth planet. One that wasn't even planned."

Tyler rapped his fist against the sheet. "With a gang of clowns like this anything could happen."

He jerked away the sheet and tossed it to the floor.

"There!" he cried. "Look here."

We crowded in and looked.

It was a cross section, or appeared to be a cross section, of a planet.

"A central core," said Tyler. "An atmosphere—"

"Earth?"

"Could be. Could be Mars or Venus."

The sheet was covered with what could have been spec notations.

"It doesn't look quite right," I protested.

"It wouldn't if it were Mars or Venus. And how sure are you of Earth?"

"Not sure at all," I said.

He jerked away the sheet to reveal another one.

We puzzled over it.

"Atmospheric profile," I guessed half-heartedly.

"These are just general specs," said Tyler. "The details will be in some of the other rolls. We have a lot of them out there."

I tried to envision it. A construction shack set down in a cloud of dust and gas. Engineers who may have worked for millennia to put together stars and planets; to key into them certain factors that still would be at work, billions of years later.

Tyler said they had bungled and perhaps they had.

But maybe not with Venus. Maybe Venus had been built to different specifications. Maybe it had been designed to be the way it was. Perhaps, a billion years from now, when humanity might well be gone from Earth, a new life and a new intelligence would rise on Venus.

Maybe not with Venus, maybe with none of the others, either. We could not pretend to know.

Tyler was still going through the sheets.

"Look here," he was yelling. "Look here—the bunglers—"

The Grotto of the Dancing Deer

Luis was playing his pipe when Boyd climbed the steep path that led up to the cave. There was no need to visit the cave again; all the work was done, mapping, measuring, photographing, extracting all possible information from the site. Not only the paintings, although the paintings were the important part of it. Also there had been the animal bones, charred, and the still remaining charcoal of the fire in which they had been charred; the small store of natural earths from which the pigments used by the painters had been compounded—a cache of valuable components, perhaps hidden by an artist who, for some reason that could not now be guessed, had been unable to use them; the atrophied human hand, severed at the wrist (why had it been severed and, once severed, left there to be found by men thirty millennia removed?); the lamp formed out of a chunk of sandstone, hollowed to accommodate a wad of moss, the hollow filled with fat, the moss serving as a wick to give light to those who painted. All these and many other things, Boyd thought with some satisfaction; Gavarnie had turned out to be, possibly because of the sophisticated scientific methods of investigation that had been brought to bear, the most significant cave painting site ever studied—perhaps not as spectacular, in some ways, as Lascaux, but far more productive in the data obtained.

No need to visit the cave again, and yet there was a reason —the nagging feeling that he had passed something up, that in the rush and his concentration on the other work, he had forgotten something. It had made small impression on him at the time, but now, thinking back on it, he was becoming more and more inclined to believe it might have importance. The whole thing probably was a product of his imagination, he told himself. Once he saw it again (if indeed he could find it again, if it were not a product of retrospective worry), it might prove to be nothing at all, simply an impression that had popped up to nag him.

So here he was again, climbing the steep path, geologist's hammer swinging at his belt, large flashlight clutched in hand, listening to the piping of Luis who perched on a small terrace, just below the mouth of the cave, a post he had occupied through all the time the work was going on. Luis had camped there in his tent through all kinds of weather, cooking on a camper's stove, serving as self-appointed watch-dog, on alert against intruders, although there had been few intruders other than the occasional curious tourist who had heard of the project and tramped miles out of the way to see it. The villagers in the valley below had been no trouble; they couldn't have cared less about what was happening on the slope above them.

Luis was no stranger to Boyd; ten years before, he had shown up at the rock shelter project some fifty miles distant and there had stayed through two seasons of digging. The rock shelter had not proved as productive as Boyd initially had hoped, although it had shed some new light on the Azilian culture, the tag-end of the great Western European prehistoric groups. Taken on as a common laborer, Luis had proved an apt pupil and as the work went on had been given greater responsibility. A week after the work had started at Gavarnie, he had shown up again.

"I heard you were here," he'd said. "What do you have for me?"

As he came around a sharp bend in the trail, Boyd saw him, sitting cross-legged in front of the weather-beaten tent, holding the primitive pipe of his to his lips, piping away.

That was exactly what it was—piping. Whatever music came out of the pipe was primitive and elemental. Scarcely music, although Boyd would admit that he knew nothing about music. Four notes—would it be four notes? he wondered. A hollow bone with an elongated slot as a mouthpiece, two drilled holes for stops.

Once he had asked Luis about it. "I've never seen anything like it," he had said. Luis had told him, "You don't see many of them. In remote villages here and there, hidden away in the mountains."

Boyd left the path and walked across the grassy terrace, sat down beside Luis, who took down the pipe and laid it in his lap.

"I thought you were gone," Luis said. "The others left a couple of days ago."

"Back for one last look," said Boyd.

"You are reluctant to leave it?"

"Yes, I suppose I am."

Below them the valley spread out in autumn browns and tans, the small river a silver ribbon in the sunlight, the red roofs of the village a splash of color beside the river.

"It's nice up here," said Boyd. "Time and time again, I catch myself trying to imagine what it might have been like at the time the paintings were done. Not much different than it is now, perhaps. The mountains would be unchanged. There'd have been no fields in the valley, but it probably would have been natural pasture. A few trees here and there, but not too many of them. Good hunting. There'd have been grass for the grazing animals. I have even tried to figure out where the people would've camped. My guess would be where the village is now."

He looked around at Luis. The man still sat upon the grass, the pipe resting in his lap. He was smiling quietly, as if he might be smiling to himself. The small black beret sat squarely on his head, his tanned face was round and smooth, the black hair close-clipped, the blue shirt open at the throat. A young man, strong, not a wrinkle on his face.

"You love your work," said Luis.

"I'm devoted to it. So are you, Luis," Boyd said.

"It's not my work."

"Your work or not," said Boyd, "you do it well. Would you like to go with me? One last look around."

"I need to run an errand in the village."

"I thought I'd find you gone," said Boyd. "I was surprised to hear your pipe."

"I'll go soon," said Luis. "Another day or two. No reason to stay but, like you, I like this place. I have no place to go, no one needing me. Nothing's lost by staying a few more days."

"As long as you like," said Boyd. "The place is yours. Before too long, the government will be setting up a caretaker arrangement, but the government moves with due deliberation."

"Then I may not see you again," said Luis.

"I took a couple of days to drive to Roncesvalles," said Boyd. "That's the place where the Gascons slaughtered Charlemagne's rearguard in 778."

"I've heard of the place," said Luis.

"I'd always wanted to see it. Never had the time. The Charlemagne chapel is in ruins, but I am told masses are still said in the village chapel for the dead paladins. When I returned from the trip, I couldn't resist the urge to see the cave again."

"I am glad of that," said Luis. "May I be impertinent?"

"You're never impertinent," said Boyd.

"Before you go, could we break bread once more together? Tonight, perhaps, I'll prepare an omelet."

Boyd hesitated, gagging down a suggestion that Luis dine with him. Then he said, "I'd be delighted, Luis. I'll bring a bottle of good wine."

Holding the flashlight centered on the rock wall, Boyd bent to examine the rock more closely. He had not imagined it; he had been right. Here, in this particular spot, the rock was not solid. It was broken into several pieces, but with the several pieces flush with the rest of the wall. Only by chance could the break have been spotted. Had he not been looking directly at it, watching for it as he swept the light across the wall, he would have missed it. It was strange, he thought, that someone else, during the time they had been working in the cave, had not found it. There'd not been much that they'd missed.

He held his breath, feeling a little foolish at the holding of it, for, after all, it might mean nothing. Frost cracks, perhaps, although he knew that he was wrong. It would be unusual to find frost cracks here.

He took the hammer out of his belt and, holding the flashlight in one hand, trained on the spot, he forced the chisel end of the hammer into one of the cracks. The edge went in easily. He pried gently and the crack widened. Under more pressure, the piece of rock moved out. He laid down the hammer and flash, seized the slab of rock and pulled it free. Beneath it were two other slabs and they both came free as easily as the first. There were others as well and he also took them out. Kneeling on the floor of the cave, he directed the light into the fissure that he had uncovered.

Big enough for a man to crawl into, but at the prospect he remained for the moment undecided. Alone, he'd be taking a chance to do it. If something happened, if he should get stuck, if a fragment of rock should shift and pin him or fall upon him, there'd be no rescue. Or probably no rescue in time to save him. Luis would come back to the camp and wait for him, but should he fail to make an appearance, Luis more than likely would take it as a rebuke for impertinence or an American's callous disregard of him. It would never occur to him that Boyd might be trapped in the cave.

Still, it was his last chance. Tomorrow he'd have to drive to Paris to catch his plane. And this whole thing was intriguing; it was not something to be ignored. The fissure must have some significance; otherwise, why should it have been walled up so carefully? Who, he wondered, would have walled it up? No one, certainly, in recent times. Anyone, finding the hidden entrance to the cave, almost immediately would have seen the paintings and would have spread the word. So the entrance to the fissure must have been blocked by one who would have been unfamiliar with the significance of the paintings or by one to whom they could have been commonplace.

It was something, he decided, that could not be passed up. He would have to go in. He secured the hammer to his belt, picked up the flashlight and began to crawl.

The fissure ran straight and easy for a hundred feet or more. It offered barely room enough for crawling, but other than that, no great difficulties. Then, without warning, it came to an end. Boyd lay in it, directing the flash beam ahead of him, staring in consternation at the smooth wall of rock that came down to cut the fissure off.

It made no sense. Why should someone go to the trouble of walling off an empty fissure? He could have missed something on the way, but thinking of it, he was fairly sure he hadn't. His progress had been slow and he had kept the flash directed ahead of him every inch of the way. Certainly if there had been anything out of the ordinary, he would have seen it.

Then a thought came to him and slowly, with some

effort, he began to turn himself around, so that his back rather than his front, lay on the fissure floor. Directing the beam upward, he had his answer. In the roof of the fissure gaped a hole.

Cautiously, he raised himself into a sitting position. Reaching up, he found handholds on the projecting rock and pulled himself erect. Swinging the flash around, he saw that the hole opened, not into another fissure, but into a bubblelike cavity—small, no more than six feet in any dimension. The walls and ceiling of the cavity were smooth, as if a bubble of plastic rock had existed here for a moment at some time in the distant geologic past when the mountains had been heaving upward leaving behind it as it drained away a bubble forever frozen into smooth and solid stone.

As he swung the flash across the bubble, he gasped in astonishment. Colorful animals capered around the entire expanse of stone. Bison played leapfrog. Horses cantered in a chorus line. Mammoths turned somersaults. All around the bottom perimeter, just above the floor, dancing deer, standing on their hind legs, joined hands and jigged, antlers swaying gracefully.

"For the love of Christ!" said Boyd.

Here was Stone Age Disney.

If it was the Stone Age. Could some jokester have crawled into the area in fairly recent times to paint the animals in this grotto? Thinking it over, he rejected the idea. So far as he had been able to ascertain, no one in the valley, nor in the entire region, for that matter, had known of the cave until a shepherd had found it several years before when a lamb had blundered into it. The entrance was small and apparently for centuries had been masked by a heavy growth of brush and bracken.

Too, the execution of the paintings had a prehistoric touch to them. Perspective played but a small part. The paintings had that curious flat look that distinguished most prehistoric art. There was no background—no horizon line, no trees, no grass or flowers, no clouds, no sense of sky. Although, he reminded himself, anyone who had any knowledge of cave painting probably would have been aware of all these factors and worked to duplicate them.

Yet, despite the noncharacteristic antics of the painted animals, the pictures did have the feeling of cave art. What ancient man, Boyd asked himself, what kind of ancient man, would have painted gamboling bison and tumbling mammoths? While the situation did not hold in all cave art, all the paintings in this particular cave were deadly serious—conservative as to form and with a forthright, honest attempt to portray the animals as the artists had seen them. There was no frivolity, not even the imprint of paint-smeared human hands as so often happened in other caves. The men who had worked in this cave had not as yet been corrupted by the symbolism that had crept in, apparently rather late in the prehistoric painting cycle.

So who had been this clown who had crept off by himself in this hidden cavern to paint his comic animals? That he had been an accomplished painter there could be no doubt. This artist's techniques and executions were without flaw.

Boyd hauled himself up through the hole, slid out onto the two-foot ledge that ran all around the hole, crouching, for there was no room to stand. Much of the painting, he realized, must have been done with the artist lying flat upon his back, reaching up to the work on the curving ceiling.

He swept the beam of the flashlight along the ledge. Halfway around, he halted the light and jiggled it back and forth to focus upon something that was placed upon the ledge, something that undoubtedly had been left by the artist when he had finished his work and gone away.

Leaning forward, Boyd squinted to make out what it was. It looked like the shoulder blade of a deer; beside the shoulder blade lay a lump of stone.

Cautiously, he edged his way around the ledge. He had been right. It was the shoulder blade of a deer. Upon the flat surface of it lay a lumpy substance. Paint? he wondered, the mixture of animal fat and mineral earths the prehistoric artists used as paints? He focused the flash closer and there was no doubt. It was paint, spread over the surface of the bone which had served as a palette, with some of the paint lying in thicker lumps ready for use, but never used, paint dried and mummified and bearing imprints of some sort. He leaned close, bringing his face down to within a few inches of the paint, shining the light upon the surface. The imprints, he saw, were fingerprints, some of them sunk deep—the signature of that ancient, long-dead man who had worked here, crouching even as Boyd now crouched, shoulders hunched against the curving stone. He put out his hand to touch the palette, then pulled it back. Symbolic, yes, this move to touch, this reaching out to touch the man who painted—but symbolic only; a gesture with too many centuries between.

He shifted the flashlight beam to the small block of stone that lay beside the shoulder blade. A lamp—hollowed-out sandstone, a hollow to hold the fat and the chunk of moss that served as a wick. The fat and wick were long since gone, but a thin film of soot still remained around the rim of the hollow that had held them.

Finishing his work, the artist had left his tools behind him, had even left the lamp, perhaps still guttering, with the fat almost finished—had left it here and let himself down into the fissure, crawling it in darkness. To him, perhaps, there was no need of light. He could crawl the tunnel by touch and familiarity. He must have crawled the route many times, for the work upon these walls had taken long, perhaps many days.

So he had left, crawling through the fissure, using the

blocks of stone to close the opening to the fissure, then had walked away, scrambling down the slope to the valley where grazing herds had lifted their heads to watch him, then had gone back to grazing.

But when had this all happened? Probably, Boyd told himself, after the cave itself had been painted, perhaps even after the paintings in the cave had lost much of whatever significance they originally would have held—one lone man coming back to paint his secret animals in his secret place. Painting them as a mockery of the pompous, magical importance of the main cave paintings? Or as a protest against the stuffy conservatism of the original paintings? Or simply as a bubbling chuckle, an exuberance of life, perhaps even a joyous rebellion against the grimness and the simplemindedness of the hunting magic? A rebel, he thought, a prehistoric rebel—an intellectual rebel? Or, perhaps, simply a man with a viewpoint slightly skewed from the philosophy of his time?

But this was that other man, that ancient man. Now how about himself? Having found the grotto, what did he do next? What would be the best way to handle it? Certainly he could not turn his back upon it and walk away, as the artist, leaving his palette and his lamp behind him, had walked away. For this was an important discovery. There could be no question of that. Here was a new and unsuspected approach to the prehistoric mind, a facet of ancient thinking that never had been guessed.

Leave everything as it lay, close up the fissure and make a phone call to Washington and another one to Paris, unpack his bags and settle down for a few more weeks of work. Get back the photographers and other members of the crew—do a job of it. Yes, he told himself, that was the way to do it.

Something lying behind the lamp, almost hidden by the sandstone lamp, glinted in the light. Something white and small.

Still crouched over, Boyd shuffled forward to get a better look.

It was a piece of bone, probably a leg bone from a small grazing animal. He reached out and picked it up and, having seen what it was, hunched unmoving over it, not quite sure what to make of it.

It was a pipe, a brother to the pipe that Luis carried in his jacket pocket, had carried in his pocket since that first day he'd met him, years ago. There was the mouthpiece slot, there the two round stops. In that long-gone day when the paintings had been done the artist had hunched here, in the flickering of the lamp, and had played softly to himself, those simple piping airs that Luis had played almost every evening, after work was done.

"Merciful Jesus," Boyd said, almost prayerfully, "it simply cannot be!"

He stayed there, frozen in his crouch, the thoughts hammering in his mind while he tried to push the thoughts away. They would not go away. He'd drive them away for just a little distance, then they'd come surging back to overwhelm him.

Finally, grimly, he broke the trance in which the thoughts had held him. He worked deliberately, forcing himself to do what he knew must be done.

He took off his windbreaker and carefully wrapped the shoulder blade palette and the pipe inside, leaving the lamp. He let himself down into the fissure and crawled, carefully protecting the bundle that he carried. In the cave again, he meticulously fitted the blocks of stone together to block the fissure mouth, scraped together handfuls of soil from the cave floor and smeared it on the face of the blocks, wiping it away, but leaving a small clinging film to mask the opening to all but the most inquiring eye.

Luis was not at his camp on the terrace below the cave mouth. He was still on his errand into the village.

When he reached his hotel, Boyd made his telephone

call to Washington. He skipped the call to Paris.

The last leaves of October were blowing in the autumn wind and a weak sun, not entirely obscured by the floating clouds, shone down on Washington.

John Roberts was waiting for him on the park bench. They nodded at one another, without speaking, and Boyd sat down beside his friend.

"You took a big chance," said Roberts. "What would have happened if the customs people. . ."

"I wasn't too worried," Boyd said. "I knew this man in Paris. For years he's been smuggling stuff into America. He's good at it and he owed me one. What have you got?"

"Maybe more than you want to hear."

"Try me."

"The fingerprints match," said Roberts.

"You were able to get a reading on the paint impressions?"

"Loud and clear."

"The FBI?"

"Yes, the FBI. It wasn't easy, but I have a friend or two."

"And the dating?"

"No problem. The bad part of the job was convincing my man this was top secret. He's still not sure it is."

"Will he keep his mouth shut?"

"I think so. Without evidence no one would believe him. It would sound like a fairy story."

"Tell me."

"Twenty-two thousand. Plus or minus three hundred years."

"And the prints do match. The bottle prints and. . ."

"I told you they match. Now will you tell me how in hell a man who lived twenty-two thousand years ago could leave his prints on a wine bottle that was manufactured last year."

"It's a long story," said Boyd. "I don't know if I should.

First, where do you have the shoulder blade?"

"Hidden," said Roberts. "Well hidden. You can have it back, and the bottle, any time you wish."

Boyd shrugged. "Not yet. Not for a while. Perhaps never."

"Never?"

"Look, John, I have to think it out."

"What a hell of a mess," said Roberts. "No one wants the stuff. No one would dare to have it. Smithsonian wouldn't touch it with a ten-foot pole. I haven't asked. They don't even know about it. But I know they wouldn't want it. There's something, isn't there, about sneaking artifacts out of a country. . ."

"Yes, there is," said Boyd.

"And now you don't want it."

"I didn't say that. I just said let it stay where it is for a time. It's safe, isn't it?"

"It's safe. And now. . ."

"I told you it is a long story. I'll try to make it short. There's this man—a Basque. He came to me ten years ago when I was doing the rock shelter. . ."

Roberts nodded. "I remember that one."

"He wanted work and I gave him work. He broke in fast, caught onto the techniques immediately. Became a valuable man. That often happens with native laborers. They seem to have the feel for their own antiquity. And then when we started work on the cave he showed up again. I was glad to see him. The two of us, as a matter of fact, are fairly good friends. On my last night at the cave he cooked a marvelous omelet—eggs, tomato, green pimentoes, onions, sausages and home-cured ham. I brought a bottle of wine."

"*The* bottle?"

"Yes, *the* bottle."

"So go ahead."

"He played a pipe. A bone pipe. A squeaky sort of thing. Not too much music in it. . ."

"There was a pipe. . ."

"Not that pipe. Another pipe. The same kind of pipe, but not the one our man has. Two pipes the same. One in a living man's pocket, the other beside the shoulder blade. There were things about this man I'm telling you of. Nothing that hit you between the eyes. Just little things. You would notice something and then, some time later, maybe quite a bit later, there'd be something else, but by the time that happened, you'd have forgotten the first incident and not tie the two together. Mostly it was that he knew too much. Little things a man like him would not be expected to know. Even things that no one knew. Bits and pieces of knowledge that slipped out of him, maybe without his realizing it. And his eyes. I didn't realize that until later, not until I'd found the second pipe and began to think about the other things. But I was talking about his eyes. In appearance he is a young man, a never-aging man, but his eyes are old. . ."

"Tom, you said he is a Basque."

"That's right."

"Isn't there some belief that the Basques may have descended from the Cro-Magnon?"

"I'm beginning to think he is."

"But think of it—twenty thousand years!"

"Yes, I know," said Boyd.

Boyd heard the piping when he reached the bottom of the trail that led up to the cave. The notes were ragged, torn by the wind. The Pyrenees stood up against the high blue sky.

Tucking the bottle of wine more securely underneath his arm, Boyd began the climb. Below him lay the redness of the village rooftops and the sere brown of autumn that spread across the valley. The piping continued, lifting and falling as the wind tugged at it playfully.

Luis sat cross-legged in front of the tattered tent.

When he saw Boyd, he put the pipe in his lap and sat waiting.

Boyd sat down beside him, handing him the bottle. Luis took it and began working on the cork.

"I heard you were back," he said. "How went the trip?"

"It went well," said Boyd.

"So now you know," said Luis.

Boyd nodded. "I think you wanted me to know. Why should you have wanted that?"

"The years grow long," said Luis. "The burden heavy. It is lonely, all alone."

"You are not alone."

"It's lonely when no one knows you. You now are the first who has really known me.

"This lifts the burden for a time," said Luis. "Once you are gone, I will be able to take it up again. And there is something. . ."

"Yes, what is it, Luis?"

"You say when you are gone there'll be no one again. Does that mean. . ."

"If what you're getting at is whether I will spread the word, no, I won't. Not unless you wish it. I have thought on what would happen to you if the world were told."

"I have certain defenses. You can't live as long as I have if you fail in your defenses."

"What kind of defenses?"

"Defenses. That is all."

"I'm sorry if I pried. There's one other thing. If you wanted me to know, you took a long chance. Why, if something had gone wrong, if I had failed to find the grotto. . ."

"I had hoped, at first, that the grotto would not be necessary. I had thought you might have guessed, on your own."

"I knew there was something wrong. But this is so outrageous I couldn't have trusted myself even had I guessed. You know it's outrageous, Luis. And if I'd not found the grotto. . . Its finding was pure chance, you know."

"If you hadn't, I would have waited. Some other time, some other year, there would have been someone else. Some other way to betray myself."

"You could have told me."

"Cold, you mean?"

"That's what I mean. I would not have believed you, of course. Not at first."

"Don't you understand? I could not have told you. The concealment now is second nature. One of the defenses I talked about. I simply could not have brought myself to tell you, or anyone."

"Why me? Why wait all these years until I came along?"

"I did not wait, Boyd. There were others, at different times. None of them worked out. I had to find, you must understand, someone who had the strength to face it. Not one who would run screaming madly. I knew you would not run screaming."

"I've had time to think it through," Boyd said. "I've come to terms with it. I can accept the fact, but not too well, only barely. Luis, do you have some explanation? How come you are so different from the rest of us?"

"No idea at all. No inkling. At one time, I thought there must be others like me and I sought for them. I found none. I no longer seek."

The cork came free and he handed the bottle of wine to Boyd. "You go first," he said steadily.

Boyd lifted the bottle and drank. He handed it to Luis. He watched him as he drank. Wondering, as he watched, how he could be sitting here, talking calmly with a man who had lived, who had stayed young through twenty thousand years. His gorge rose once again against acceptance of the fact—but it had to be a fact. The shoulder blade, the small amount of organic matter still remaining in the pigment, had measured out to twenty-two thousand years. There was no question that the prints in the paint had matched the prints upon the bottle. He had raised one question back in Washington, hoping there might be evidence of hoax. Would it have been possible, he had asked, that the ancient pigment, the paint used by the prehistoric artist, could have been reconstituted, the fingerprints impressed upon it, and then replaced in the grotto? Impossible was the answer. Any reconstitution of the pigment, had it been possible, would have shown up in the analysis. There had been nothing of the sort—the pigment dated to twenty thousand years ago. There was no question of that.

"All right, Cro-Magnon," said Boyd, "tell me how you did it. How does a man survive as long as you have? You do not age, of course. Your body will not accept disease. But I take it you are not immune to violence or to accident. You've lived in a violent world. How does a man sidestep accident and violence for two hundred centuries?"

"There were times early," Luis said, "when I came close to not surviving. For a long time, I did not realize the kind of thing I was. Sure, I lived longer, stayed younger than all the others—I would guess, however, that I didn't begin to notice this until I began to realize that all the people I had known in my early life were dead—dead for a long, long time. I knew then that I was different from the rest. About the same time others began to notice I was different. They became suspicious of me. Some of them resented me. Others thought I was some sort of evil spirit. Finally I had to flee the tribe. I became a skulking outcast. That was when I began to learn the principles of survival."

"And those principles?"

"You keep a low profile. You don't stand out. You attract no attention to yourself. You cultivate a cowardly attitude. You are never brave. You take no risks. You let others do the dirty work. You never volunteer. You skulk and run and hide. You grow a skin that's thick; you don't give a damn what others think of you. You shed all your noble attributes, your social consciousness. You shuck your loyalty to tribe or folk or country. You're not a patriot. You live for yourself alone. You're an observer, never a participant. You scuttle around the edges of things. And you become so self-centered that you come to believe that no blame should attach to you, that you are living in the only logical way a man can live. You went to Roncesvalles the other day, remember?"

"Yes. I mentioned I'd been there. You said you'd heard of it."

"Heard of it. Hell, I was there the day it happened—August 15th, 778. An observer, not a participant. A cowardly little bastard who tagged along behind the noble band of Gascons who did in Charlemagne. Gascons, hell. That's the fancy name for them. They were Basques, pure and simple. The meanest crew of men who ever drew the breath of life. Some Basques may be noble, but not this band. Not the kind of warriors who'd stand up face to face with the Franks. They hid up in the pass and rolled rocks down on all those puissant knights. But it wasn't the knights who held their interest. It was the wagon train. They weren't out to fight a war or to avenge a wrong. They were out for loot. Although little good it did them."

"Why do you say that?"

"It was this way," said Luis. "They knew the rest of the Frankish army would return when the rearguard didn't come up and they had not the stomach for that. They stripped the dead knights of their golden spurs, their armor and fancy clothes, the money bags they carried and loaded all of it on the wagons and got out of there. A few miles further on, deep in the mountains, they holed up and hid. In a deep canyon where they thought they would be safe. But if they should be found, they had what amounted to a fort. A half mile or so below the place they camped, the canyon narrowed and twisted sharply. A lot of boulders had fallen down at that point, forming a barricade that could have been held by a handful of men against any assault that could be launched against it. By this time, I was a long way off. I smelled something wrong, I knew something most unpleasant was about to happen. That's another thing about this survival business. You develop special senses. You get so you can smell out trouble, well ahead of time. I heard what happened later."

He lifted the bottle and had another drink. He handed it to Boyd.

"Don't leave me hanging," said Boyd. "Tell me what did happen."

"In the night," said Luis, "a storm came up. One of those sudden, brutal summer thunderstorms. This time it was a cloudburst. My brave fellow Gascons died to the man. That's the price of bravery."

Boyd took a drink, lowered the bottle, held it to his chest, cuddling it.

"You know about this," he said. "No one else does. Perhaps no one had ever wondered what happened to those Gascons who gave Charlemagne the bloody nose. You must know of other things. Christ, man, you've lived history. You didn't stick to this area."

"No. At times I wandered. I had an itching foot. There were things to see. I had to keep moving along. I couldn't stay in one place any length of time or it would be noticed that I wasn't aging."

"You lived through the Black Death," said Boyd. "You watched the Roman legions. You heard first hand of Attila. You skulked along on Crusades. You walked the streets of ancient Athens."

"Not Athens," said Luis. "Somehow Athens was never to my taste. I spent some time in Sparta. Sparta, I tell you—that was really something."

"You're an educated man," said Boyd. "Where did you go to school?"

"Paris, for a time, in the fourteenth century. Later on at Oxford. After that at other places. Under different names. Don't try tracing me through the schools that I attended."

"You could write a book," said Boyd. "It would set new sales records. You'd be a millionaire. One book and you'd be a millionaire."

"I can't afford to be a millionaire. I can't be noticed and millionaires are noticed. I'm not in want. I've never been in want. There's always treasure for a skulker to pick up. I have caches here and there. I get along all right."

Luis was right, Boyd told himself. He couldn't be a millionaire. He couldn't write a book. In no way could he be famous, stand out in any way. In all things, he must remain unremarkable, always anonymous.

The principles of survival, he had said. And this part of it, although not all of it. He had mentioned the art of smelling trouble, the hunch ability. There would be, as well, the wisdom, the street savvy, the cynicism that a man would pick up along the way, the expertise, the ability to judge character, an insight into human reaction, some knowledge concerning the use of power, power of every sort, economic power, political power, religious power.

Was the man still human, he wondered, or had he, in twenty thousand years, become something more than human? Had he advanced that one vital step that would place him beyond humankind, the king of being that would come after man?

"One thing more," said Boyd. "Why the Disney paintings?"

"They were painted some time later than the others," Luis told him. "I painted some of the earlier stuff in the cave. The fishing bear is mine. I knew about the grotto. I found it and said nothing. No reason I should have kept it secret. Just one of those little items one hugs to himself to make himself important. I know something you don't know—silly stuff like that. Later I came back to paint the grotto. The cave art was so deadly serious. Such terribly silly magic. I told myself painting should be fun. So I came back, after the tribe had moved and painted simply for the fun of it. How did it strike you, Boyd?"

"Damn good art," said Boyd.

"I was afraid you wouldn't find the grotto and I couldn't help you. I knew you had seen the cracks in the wall; I watched you one day looking at them. I counted on your remembering them. And I counted on you seeing the fingerprints and finding the pipe. All pure serendipity, of course. I had nothing in mind when I left the paint with the fingerprints and the pipe. The pipe, of course, was the tip-off and I was confident you'd at least be curious. But I couldn't be sure. When we ate that night, here by the campfire, you didn't mention the grotto and I was afraid you'd blown it. But when you made off with the bottle, sneaking it away, I knew I had it made. And now the big question. Will you let the world in on the grotto paintings?"

"I don't know. I'll have to think about it. What are your thoughts on the matter?"

"I'd just as soon you didn't."

"Okay," said Boyd. "Not for the time at least. Is there anything else I can do for you? Anything you want?"

"You've done the best thing possible," said Luis. "You know who I am, what I am. I don't know why that's so important to me, but it is. A matter of identity, I suppose. When you die, which I hope will be a long time from now, then, once again, there'll be no one who knows. But the knowledge that one man did know, and what is more important, understood, will sustain me through the centuries. A minute—I have something for you."

He rose and went into the tent, came back with a sheet of paper, handing it to Boyd. It was a topographical survey of some sort.

"I've put a cross on it," said Luis. "To mark the spot."

"What spot?"

"Where you'll find the Charlemagne treasure of Roncesvalles. The wagons and the treasure would have been carried down the canyon in the flood. The turn in the canyon and the boulder barricade I spoke of would have blocked them. You'll find them there, probably under a deep layer of gravel and debris."

Boyd looked up questioningly from the map.

"It's worth going after," said Luis. "Also it provides another check against the validity of my story."

"I believe you," said Boyd. "I need no further evidence."

"Ah, well," said Luis, "it wouldn't hurt! And now, it's time to go."

"Time to go! We have a lot to talk about."

"Later, perhaps," said Luis. "We'll bump into one another from time to time. I'll make a point we do. But now it's time to go."

He started down the path and Boyd sat watching him.

After a few steps, Luis halted and half-turned back to Boyd.

"It seems to me," he said in explanation, "it's always time to go."

Boyd stood and watched him move down the trail toward the village. There was about the moving figure a deep sense of loneliness—the most lonely man in all the world.

STATEMENT OF LIMITATION

Over the River and Through the Woods by Clifford D. Simak has been published in a limited edition hardcover edition of 874 copies and in a special deluxe, leather-bound edition, autographed by Poul Anderson and numbered 1-100. A further boxed, deluxe leather-bound edition, autographed by Poul Anderson, is lettered A-Z.